FATHER DAMIEN AND THE BELLS

FATHER DAMIEN
AND THE BELLS

Written by Arthur and Elizabeth Odell Sheehan

ILLUSTRATED BY LEONARD EVERETT FISHER

IGNATIUS PRESS   SAN FRANCISCO

First edition published by Farrar, Straus and Cudahy, Inc., New York
Published with ecclesiastical approval
Published by arrangement with
Farrar, Straus and Giroux, LLC

Cover art by Christopher J. Pelicano
Cover design by Riz Boncan Marsella

Published in 2004 by Ignatius Press, San Francisco
ISBN 978-1-58617-033-2
Library of Congress Control Number 2004103526

Manufactured by Thomson-Shore, Dexter, MI (USA); RMA578LS798, December, 2011 ∞

For Mary Agnes and Elizabeth Anne

CONTENTS

Foreword

In the tower of Saint Rombaut's cathedral, in the Belgian city of Malines, hangs a family of bells. There are forty-nine of them altogether, forming one of the world's most famous carillons. For more than a century, travelers have stopped at Malines especially to hear the glorious music of the bells when the carillonneur sets them ringing in their tower. Each bell has its own blessing, its own name. Each has its own voice, high, clear, and pealing or low, thunderous, and tolling. And the deepest voice of all belongs to the biggest bell, whose name is Salvator.

Like pebbles making circles in water, the bells have always made circles of sound that widen out past the Malines marketplace, with its rows of carts, and down the beech-shaded streets. There they ring over the white-capped heads of the lacemakers, bending over their twisting bobbins, and over the sharp, pointed rooftops. Finally, they ring out beyond the wharves in the busy harbor, out over the fresh-smelling gardens of strawberry and asparagus, and into the open country.

Because Flanders has no hills to stop it, the bell sound goes out along the flat, dusty, cobbled roads, in and out through the red and blue wagons and dogcarts, among the quiet rivers that weave between curved and grassy banks. Finally, the music is wound into a tight skein of song on the huge bare arms of the windmills.

Saint Rombaut's bells were already ringing when Joseph de Veuster was born. His birth was on January 3, 1840, in a farmhouse at Tremeloo, not very far down the road from Malines, the same road that Salvator's bass voice so often traveled.

Flanders is a land of bells, and Joseph de Veuster was to know and love their pealing all his life. Many bells would ring for him: monastery bells, paced into prayerful silence; ship's bells, marking time across two oceans; tinny chapel bells, clanging madly in a tropical earthquake; the almost soundless tinkle of a tiny Communion bell in a darkened room; and, finally, Saint Rombaut's again, flinging a mighty peal of triumph across the world, even to the bitter gray cliffs of an island once known as Godforsaken.

I

A FIRESIDE IN FLANDERS

"JEF! JEF! Where are you now?"

Mrs. de Veuster closed the door of her white-shuttered cottage and started down the path toward the road. She looked around at her children standing by the wagon. Yes, all the rest were there.

Suddenly, her youngest son ran around the corner of the house.

"Where have you been, Jef?" His mother looked him over a bit anxiously. "Not getting your new suit all dirty, I hope!"

"Just visiting my lamb." The little boy turned blue eyes to his mother and smiled. She always found it hard to scold Jef when he smiled like that. "I thought maybe it got cold last night."

"Even on fair day he can't forget that old lamb!" Pauline spoke in her older-sister voice, looking down at chubby Jef. He always had some pet among the farm animals.

"Into the wagon, now, all of you, or we'll be late for Mass!" Mr. de Veuster, sitting on the wagon seat, gave the reins an impatient tug. He looked very dignified in his good black suit.

They all piled in for the two-mile drive to the village of Werchter. Leonce and Gerard, the two oldest boys, sat together. Pauline helped her mother arrange her cloak. Jef and Auguste chattered excitedly of what they would do at the fair. As they drove into Werchter, the bells of Saint John the Baptist church were ringing; they had just time to take their places before the Solemn High Mass began.

It was the Feast of Pentecost, always celebrated in Flemish villages by a *kermesse*, or fair. After Mass, Jef and the others hurried to find a good place to watch the procession. The statues from the church were borne out triumphantly and carried along the main street. The men of the parish marched proudly, holding high their bright-colored banners. For the de Veusters and their neighbors, accustomed to the quiet, hard-working routine of farm life, the *kermesse* was a joyous, even thrilling, event. Families were united for the day—cousins, aunts, uncles, and grandparents all sharing together the excitement of the occasion.

After the procession, the real fun began. In the marketplace, merchants spread their wares temptingly, to be admired and sometimes bought, by the frugal Flemish women, still wearing their dark-colored, everyday dresses, for most were too poor to buy holiday attire. But if their clothes were somber, their spirits were not, for no true Fleming ever brought any sorrow with him to the *kermesse*!

For the men, who prided themselves on their robust physical strength and agility, there were games of skill—archery and shooting—and plenty of good, dark, Flemish beer, the national drink.

Jef wanted to go on the merry-go-round drawn by donkeys, while the older boys joined in the sack races and other games. There was great commotion in the usually peaceful square, as men talked and argued, sometimes in heated tones, and children laughed and shouted. Singers tried to make themselves heard over the hubbub, for they had made up special songs for this day. On one corner, a jolly juggler, surrounded by a cheering crowd, performed his tricks tirelessly.

Suddenly, a trumpet sounded, and Mrs. de Veuster turned to watch its owner, a wandering merchant in town for the fair, extolling the wonders of the medicine he was selling. She pushed her way toward the brightly decorated booth to hear more of the magical powers of this herb. After a few minutes, she noticed that Jef was not with her. Just like him, she thought, glancing around the crowded booth, to be playing a trick. He must be hiding somewhere nearby, pretending to be lost.

She called the other children to help her look for Jef. It would not be hard for a five-year-old to get lost on a day like this.

"Maybe he's with your father", Mrs. de Veuster said at last. "Auguste, go and see."

Auguste ran to the outdoor table where Mr. de Veuster and some of the neighborhood men were discussing the ups and downs of the grain business. Francis de Veuster sold grain in the nearby towns of Malines, Antwerp, and Brussels. He usually had news of the markets for the local farmers.

"Have you seen Jef? Is he with you?" Auguste was out of breath from running.

"No, he hasn't been here." Mr. de Veuster called out in his loudest voice, "Je—ef! Je—ef!"

A few tables away, a man stopped in the middle of a story, left his companions, and hurried over.

"What's the matter? Jef lost?" It was Joseph Goovaerts, Joseph's godfather. An old soldier, he loved to spend his time at the *kermesse* telling war tales, and, though his companions probably had heard the stories many times before, over a freshly drawn mug of beer the tales sounded as good as new every fair day.

"Stay where you are. I'll find the boy. Leave him to me. I know Jef. Isn't he my own namesake?" Mr. Goovaerts' voice boomed over the noise of the crowd. It was never hard to hear what he had to say.

Off he strode through the crowd of people, hardly noticing them. He did not make the rounds of the booths, as the de Veuster family had done. He did not even look from side to side, as he pushed his way through the busy square.

Turning his back on the fair altogether, he went down the quiet street leading to the church of Saint John the Baptist. It was silent and empty now, the incense from morning Mass still hanging in the air. The only light came from the lamp in the sanctuary and the few candles left burning. Mr. Goovaerts stood, peering down the shadowy aisle, searching the dimness with his sharp eye.

At first he saw nothing. But, as his eyes grew used to the gloom, he noticed a small figure kneeling close to the altar. Smiling to himself, Mr. Goovaerts went down the aisle and put his big hand lightly on the small boy's shoulder. Jef turned quickly, then rose and looked up questioningly, as his godfather steered him firmly out into the sunlit street. Jef wondered if he would get a scolding for running away from the family.

"We missed you, my boy", Mr. Goovaerts told him. "So you ran away from the fair, eh? Well—I knew where to find you, didn't I?"

"Yes, Uncle Joseph." Jef smiled now, for he saw his godfather was not angry with him.

"I knew what I was doing when I picked your name for you—yes, the very day you were born I told them you were to be called Joseph."

"Saint Joseph saved your life, didn't he, Uncle?" Jef was glad to change the subject.

"That he did, my boy, and more than once, when I was fighting in the wars", agreed the old soldier heartily.

"I wasn't lost, Uncle", said the boy.

"Not a bit of it, Jef. You have too sensible a head on you for that. Come along with me, now." Mr. Goovaerts led Jef across the square straight to where the fried-potato wagon was sending out its delicious smell.

"How many fried potatoes do you think you could eat now, Jef?" asked Uncle Joseph.

"Oh—about a thousand!" Jef was starved.

Mr. Goovaerts made sure his godson had his fill before the de Veusters climbed into the bumpy market wagon to go back to their Tremeloo farm.

Fair day came several times each year, but for the rest of the time life at Tremeloo was quiet. Like other farmers of Flanders, Mr. de Veuster had to work long and hard in the grain fields that stretched right up to the back wall of his house. All the boys had their special jobs to do, even Jef. Best of all, he liked tending the sheep. "Little shepherd", they called him.

By the time he was seven, Jef was starting out every

morning for Mr. Bols' little school in Werchter, with Pauline and Auguste, two years older.

One afternoon, as they walked home after school, they were holding hands, stretched out in a line across the road.

Suddenly, they reached a sharp bend, and from the other side a wagon was upon them in an instant. The others ducked quickly, sprawling into the ditch, but Jef was not quick enough. Struck by the wagon, he lay stunned in the road as a wheel passed over him.

Auguste was horrified. He scrambled to his feet and ran home as fast as he could.

"Come—come quick", he yelled to his mother. "Jef's hurt!"

Not even stopping to take off her apron, Mrs. de Veuster followed Auguste out the door. They took a shortcut through the fields. Jef still lay in the road, his eyes closed, very quiet.

Mrs. de Veuster picked him up gently and carried him back home. As she laid him down in his bed, he opened his eyes for a moment. "My head hurts", he said.

His mother laid a cold, wet cloth across Jef's forehead. Then she sat down beside him. She could not be sure yet how badly he was hurt.

Jef soon opened his eyes again. "What happened?" He sat up and looked around. "Ouch!" He put his hand to his head. He had a bump, all right, a big one.

"Rest a while, Jef", his mother urged

"No, I'm all right now. I want to get up. Is it supper

time?" Mrs. de Veuster saw he could not be seriously hurt.

"How could this be?" she thought, as she went back to her work. She looked at Jef, busy playing as if nothing at all had happened. Yet she knew that the wheel of the wagon had actually gone over him! She glanced at the crucifix that hung in the corner of the kitchen.

"Thank you, God", she said simply.

Jef was a bright boy. At least, that's what Mr. Bols, his teacher, said. But sometimes he had trouble keeping his mind on the lessons. Unlike Auguste, who seemed to feel at home with books, Jef had to work hard at his sums and spelling. One morning, he found lessons particularly long. He knew that Pauline, who always was in charge of the lunch, had brought to school in her canvas bag a special treat. Usually they had bread-and-butter sandwiches to eat during the noon recess. But today—Jef's mouth watered as he thought of the delicious, crunchy, sweet buns his mother had given them that morning. Would lunchtime ever come?

Finally, the bell rang. Jef ran out into the school yard. Pauline was already opening the bag.

"Here, Jef." She passed the first cake to him. "You're always the hungriest. Auguste, you're next; take this one. And don't gobble it all up in one bite." She looked sternly at her younger brothers.

"Look who's here." A boy sauntered up to them, his hands in his somewhat ragged pockets.

"Looking for us, Sus Baal? What's up?" Auguste said.

Sus Baal was not known as the best-behaved boy in the neighborhood. In fact, whenever there was mischief, he was always close by. Now he smiled as he swaggered before the three de Veusters.

"Guess what? I stopped at your house this morning. I left something for you." His eye caught the delicious cake Jef was just about to bite into.

"What was it?" Jef asked.

"Magpies", replied Sus. "Caught them myself. I thought you'd like to have them."

Jef stopped, the cake halfway to his lips.

"Magpies, did you say? Well, one good turn deserves another. Here—take my cake!"

The hand of Sus Baal was out of his pocket in a flash. He snatched the cake hungrily. He had sampled Mrs. de Veuster's baking before.

"You can have one of mine, too", Auguste offered, not wanting to be outdone by his brother's generosity.

Pauline was the last, and most unwilling. "And mine." She held out her cake.

"Here, I have a good idea", Jef said. "Why not give him all our cakes?" He saw that the boy was really hungry.

"All right, take them, then." Pauline handed over the bag, and the three children went back to the afternoon classes with very empty stomachs. Sus Baal ran off, happy as a lark, laughing and very much pleased with himself!

That afternoon, when Jef came home, he ran to the kitchen.

"Where are the magpies, Mother?" He tossed his schoolbag on the big table.

"Magpies? What are you talking about, Jef?"

"Sus Baal told us he left some birds here."

"Not a bit of it!" answered Mrs. de Veuster. "I haven't even seen that rogue today. You should know better than to believe him!"

"And what do you think Jef made us do, Mother?" spoke up Pauline. "He made us give our lunch to that bad boy—every crumb!"

"Is that right, Jef?" His mother knew her son's quick kindness as well as she knew his quick temper. She loved him all the more for his impulsive nature.

"I did *not* make them." Jef's eyes flashed as he defended himself stoutly. "I just thought it was a good idea. Besides, your cakes are so good, and I know he's always hungry!"

Mrs. de Veuster had gone to the cupboard. Now she came back with a plate of the same delicious cakes.

"Here, then", she said, as she set the dish on the table before Jef. "Take these. You must all be starved. Here's all that's left of yesterday's baking!"

The older boys spent most of the time helping their father with farm work in the late afternoon, while Auguste and Joseph studied their lessons in the cosy kitchen. The firelight from the hearth glistened and danced on the round copper pots that hung on the walls. Pauline helped her mother with the supper.

Sometimes, before the others had come in from the fields, Jef would shut his schoolbook impatiently.

"Read us a story, Mother", he would say.

"Yes, please read to us." Auguste would put his book away, too. There was nothing the children liked better than to hear a story.

Mrs. de Veuster would brush the crumbs from the table, dry her hands carefully, and go to the shelf to take down the tremendous book. It had to be carried very carefully, for it had been a priceless possession of the de Veuster family longer than anyone could remember.

The book was called *The Lives of the Holy Martyrs and Hermits*. Mrs. de Veuster was the only one in the family who could read the old-fashioned Flemish words printed in strange-looking Gothic type.

Pauline would sit by the fire, and Auguste and Joseph would crowd close to their mother as she spread out the huge volume. They loved to hear the stories of the Roman martyrs, cruelly tortured by wild beasts, and the brave but futile exploits of the Crusaders. Especially they liked to hear about the desert fathers, those saintly early Christians who led lives of poverty and penance far from cities and villages and who became the forerunners of the great religious orders of monks.

"Read the Saint Anthony one." This was Jef's favorite, and he leaned over to study the beautiful pictures as Mrs. de Veuster turned the pages slowly.

He already knew the story well—how Anthony, as a young man, had heard the stirring words in a sermon:

"If you would be perfect, go, sell what you possess."
Anthony went, and in a cave near his native village of
Coma he had prayed and fasted for fifteen years.

"Strange beasts and wild demons came to attack him
often and rained blows upon him, at times leaving him
half-dead. But he withstood them with heroic fortitude.

"Later he shut himself in a fort on the mountain of
Pispir, across the Nile River, and though he saw no one
for twenty years, many disciples came and lived in huts
and caves nearby. Finally, after coming out of his hermit-
age to teach his followers for five years, he went away to
his final retreat in the inner desert between the Nile and
the Red Sea. And here the monastery still stands upon
the mountainside, named for him, Der Mar Antonios,
because he lived there forty-five years."

This tale never ceased to fascinate Jef. He thought he,
too, would like to be a hermit and spend his days and
nights in prayer. Jef's playmates around Tremeloo knew
him as a boy who loved companionship and usually won
at games. But they knew, too, that sometimes he could
be very silent, thinking of far-off things.

One night, after hearing the story of Saint Anthony
once more, Jef had a wonderful idea. As he and Auguste
lay in their beds in the room they shared upstairs in
the farmhouse, he whispered: "Listen, Auguste, I'd
like to be a hermit, too, like Saint Anthony, wouldn't
you?"

Auguste was a serious boy, but he did not have Jef's
bold imagination.

"Yes," he answered, "but we're not old enough. The desert is too far away."

"We don't need a real desert", Jef answered, sitting up in bed in the dark room. "I don't mean that. I mean right here in the woods. We can pray there just as well."

"But when?" Auguste wanted to know.

"Tomorrow", Jef told him. "We'll get Pauline and Henri to go, too." Henri Winokx, Jef's cousin, lived with the de Veusters.

Next day the four children went off quietly. In the forest of Ninde, near Tremeloo, they found just the right spot. At noon they ate, in silence, the lunch they had brought for school. Unlike Saint Anthony's retreat, this one had no wild animals to disturb their meditation.

Still, as the sun began to go down, even Jef felt very tired. His knees hurt from kneeling on the rough ground, and the Egyptian desert did not seem half so pleasant as the de Veuster kitchen. The firelight would be playing on the walls, and the family would soon be gathering for dinner around the big table.

But Jef knew that Saint Anthony would never have given in to such a temptation. Steadfastly, he put it out of his mind.

Meanwhile, his mother was wondering about the children. Not to be home from school by nightfall was very unusual indeed! She looked anxiously down the road that led to town. Not a sign of them anywhere. Had something gone wrong? Perhaps one of them had been hurt.

When her husband came in and found the children missing, he set out immediately with the older boys, Leonce and Gerard, to find them.

A search of the neighborhood was begun, and finally the little group was discovered. They had been almost as alone in the forest of Ninde as Anthony had been on his mountainside fortress, but, when they were found, things took a very different turn.

Very unceremoniously, the children were hauled off home by Mr. de Veuster, his displeasure showing plainly in his eyes. He had no objection to hermits, in their places, but he wanted none of them around his house. His point was driven home by a sound whacking for each of the culprits. They were sent off to bed in disgrace.

Lying in his upstairs room, still feeling the sting of his father's hand and the sharp edge of his words, Jef heard Auguste crying.

"Don't cry, Auguste", he said softly. "Father doesn't really mean it, even when he's as angry as he is tonight. Anyway, the whole thing was my idea, not yours!"

"That's not why I'm crying", Auguste answered in a whisper. "It's because—well, today wasn't real. It was only play!"

"You mean", Jef wanted to know, "you want to be like Eugenie when you grow up?" Eugenie was the elder girl in the family. Jef hardly remembered this sister of his because he had been only three years old when she had left home to become a nun in Holland.

"No, not like Eugenie", Auguste replied firmly, his tears forgotten. "I will be a priest—a missionary—and go to far-off lands."

To Auguste it was not just a game. Already he was almost certain God was calling him to the religious life.

As for Jef, he, too, wanted to see what lay beyond the calm and level plains of Flanders. On a visit to nearby Malines with his father, he had seen the wharves of that busy port city crowded with ships of many lands, flying their flags of different colors.

Traveling to strange lands—becoming another Saint Anthony—these might be the dreams of any boy with a lively imagination and love for adventure.

With Auguste it was different. His words had the sound of decision.

Jef pulled up the bed covers in silence.

2

DECISION OF A CHAMPION

RACE YOU to the mill, Henri?" Jef called to his cousin. The two were skating on the frozen River Dyle that ran close to their home. Jef's cheeks were red from the frosty wind and the exercise.

"All right, come on." Henri set off, Jef close behind, the wooden runners of their skates creaking over the thick ice.

Along between the snow-covered banks they sped toward the old mill near the de Veuster farmhouse.

"Watch out for the bridge", Jef yelled. They were coming to one of the low bridges that crossed the river here and there. Henri slowed up for a moment, hunching his shoulders and ducking his head low.

Just then Jef leaped into the air, crouched down like a skier on a steep slope, and sailed under the bridge and out ahead of Henri on the other side. His long, easy strides easily outdistanced his cousin's pace.

"I won! I won!" Jef called out over his shoulder, as he slid past the finish point and whirled around suddenly.

"Oh, you always do, Jef! If you weren't my cousin, I'd say you didn't play fair." Henri smiled, for he was a good loser. Besides, he hadn't really expected to win. Nobody ever won a skating race when Joseph de Veuster was around!

"What do you mean?" Jef wanted to know. "Of course I played fair."

"You weren't skating. You were flying!"

"Come on! Let's race back again!" Jef shouted.

"Not now", Henri told him, as he sat down on the snowy riverbank and unstrapped his skates. "I have to go in now. See you later!"

Flinging his skates over his shoulder, Henri set out across the field.

Jef turned and started back down the river. He loved skating like this. It really was like flying, he imagined, with the wind at his back, helping him glide along. The countryside stretched out white and level, the clumps of firwood and willow black against the snow. Along the winding course of the Dyle River, he passed white cottages with thatched roofs or red-tiled ones, like his own.

Suddenly, Jef felt the ice give way under his foot. Lost in his own thoughts, he had come to the place where the Dyle met with the small Laak River. He had forgotten that where the two currents came together the ice was not solid. He felt himself going through!

With a mighty lurch that wrenched all the muscles in his strong body, Jef threw himself to the other side to avoid the break.

He lost his balance and fell, but he landed on thick ice a few feet away. His skates dug the glassy surface as he picked himself up, cautiously fighting for a safe footing. Standing up once more, he made straight for the bank and sat down to get his breath.

He was sore and bruised from the fall, but that was nothing to what might have happened had he gone through!

"That was close!" he said to himself, somewhat shakily. "If I hadn't swerved away in time—" He didn't like to think of that!

It was not the first close brush he had had with danger. He remembered the time he had fallen under the wheels of the moving wagon on the Werchter road. Then, too, he had narrowly escaped serious injury, even death.

"God is good to me", thought Jef, as he stood up and brushed some of the hard-packed snow from his heavy jacket. "I wonder if he has some special work for me to do!"

For four years, since he had finished the course at the Werchter village school, Joseph had been his father's right-hand helper on the farm. He was almost a young man now, and even his nickname, Jef, was seldom heard outside the family home.

"He's as good as four ordinary boys", Mr. de Veuster would say proudly, glad to have such a stalwart son to share the burdens at home. It never mattered how heavy or unpleasant the job was; Joseph was ready and able to do it!

But Mr. de Veuster was uneasy about his son's future, as he watched Joseph loading heavy sacks of grain and hauling them off in the wagon through the fields.

Handy though the boy was at all the farm tasks, his father did not think Joseph's life work was to be there at Tremeloo. Auguste had already gone off to the minor seminary; Pauline and the other two boys were still at home.

"I have Leonce and Gerard to help me here", he said to his wife. "The three of us can handle it well enough. But Joseph—he's different. There should be something special for him."

Mrs. de Veuster was not at all disturbed.

"Don't worry about him, Francis", she insisted. Joseph was special, no doubt about that. She did not mention to her husband what she had learned only the day before—that for some months her son had been sleeping on a hard board he had somehow hidden in his bed. This would anger Mr. de Veuster. Besides, she herself had scolded Joseph for taking upon himself such a penance.

One day, as Joseph was nearing his eighteenth birthday, he came in from afternoon chores to find Joseph Goovaerts, his godfather, sitting at the big kitchen table. Mr. de Veuster, his account book spread out before him, looked more serious than ever.

"And how's my favorite godson today?" boomed the old soldier. Joseph's godfather was a frequent visitor at Tremeloo.

"Very well, thanks, Uncle Joseph." Jef took off his jacket and hung it behind the door.

"Your father here has been telling me what a fine farmer you're turning out to be!"

"Oh, I like it, Uncle. Especially building. I can handle a hammer and saw pretty well now. If you want a new house in Antwerp, let me know, and I'll come and build it for you!" Joseph smiled, and his blue eyes twinkled.

Mr. de Veuster looked up. He was not smiling.

"We've just been talking about you, Joseph", he began.

"How about coming up to Antwerp and joining me in the grain business, my boy?" asked Mr. Goovaerts. "We could have some good times together, Jef. That is," and he smiled slyly, "if you don't think you'd like to become a professional boxer! How about it?"

Mr. Goovaerts had often encouraged Joseph in games and sports and was proud of his godson's athletic ability.

"I've decided we need another businessman in the family, Joseph", his father told him. "You have a good head on you and could carry on the grain trade for us."

No one in the house ever questioned Francis de Veuster's decisions. Joseph now did not show any great surprise at this turn of events.

"If that's what you think I should do—" He paused.

"Yes, it's all settled. First you must learn to speak French. Our Flemish tongue is little used in the business world, you know. Before you go to Antwerp, you'll go back to school for a while."

"To school?" Joseph had thought this part of his life was over. After all, he had not been to school in four years.

"Yes. I've gone over my accounts here very carefully, and I think I can manage to pay your way to the academy in Braine-le-Comte." Mr. de Veuster pointed to the figures on the sheet before him. "We'll go there tomorrow and make all the arrangements."

Not long afterward, Joseph found himself on the train rattling toward the town of Braine-le-Comte, in the province of Hainault, in southern Belgium. At some point in his journey, as he sat stiffly in his new suit and shiny shoes, his suitcase on the floor beside the seat, Joseph passed over the unseen boundary that cuts Belgium in two.

In his country there were few fences. The little farms were divided from one another by furrows, like lines drawn by a giant pencil. Between northern Belgium and southern Belgium lay an even less-visible barrier— a barrier of language. In Flanders, to the north, bordering Holland and the North Sea, people spoke Flemish. In Wallonia, bordering France, people spoke French. There was an age-old rivalry between the Flemish and the Walloons. But politically they were all Belgians, ready to join forces and forget differences if their country was endangered.

Joseph knew it would not be easy for him during his first days at Braine-le-Comte. He felt a little uncomfortable in his good clothes as he made his way up to the school.

"Watch this, fellows!" A short, stocky boy stood on the steps, as Joseph came up the walk with his worn and bulging suitcase. Three boys standing nearby turned to watch the newcomer, too.

"You there—what's your name?" called one in a mocking voice.

They knew he was a Fleming, and a farmer at that! His clothes, his heavy step—everything about him told them he must be a country boy.

"Joseph de Veuster", the stranger replied to their question.

"What's that again", they shouted back at him. "What did you say your name was?" They spoke in French, but he knew enough of that language to understand the question.

"Joseph de Veuster", he said again.

"What's the matter? Can't you talk plainly?" The boys laughed unkindly. Yes, he was a real Fleming, all right, with a funny accent, and probably not too bright.

"Where did you get that suit—Paris?" called the boy who had spoken to him first. It amused them to make fun of this dull-witted northerner. Joseph stopped suddenly in front of them and put down his bag.

"Well, what's wrong with it?" He returned their jeering looks with his steady, fearless gaze.

They had expected him to be cowed by their attack. Instead, he seemed to be challenging them, but he said nothing more.

Suddenly one of the boys broke from the crowd.

"Come on, let him have it!" he shouted. Joseph felt a sharp jab of pain where the other fellow's fist had struck his jaw. He saw that it was the boy who had first called out to him.

The blows were coming thick and fast. Joseph stood still only for a moment. Then a shout went up from the rest as the Walloon suddenly reeled back, dizzied by a direct punch. Around Tremeloo nobody who once had felt that fist ever came back for more. The boy paused now, noticing for the first time the stranger's broad shoulders inside his somewhat tight-fitting coat. He decided very quickly not to bother this new boy anymore. Maybe he was not so slow and dull as the rest of the northerners! All the others were now quite openly admiring Joseph's skillful self-defense.

A friendly smile quickly replaced Joseph's stern look.

He put out his hand—the same one he had just used to deliver a reeling blow.

"I said—my name's Joseph. Joseph de Veuster—champion boxer of Ninde!"

This time no one jeered. The other boy put out his hand, too.

"I'm Antoine", he said. "Come on. I'll take you to the headmaster."

The knees of Joseph's new pants were torn that first day. After that, there were a few more bruised knuckles and sore jaws, but gradually the Walloon students stopped teasing him. He showed them very quickly that he could defend himself only too well! Little by little, as he learned to speak their language, Joseph made friends at Braine-le-Comte.

"I have a nice clean room and plenty of good food," he wrote home, "and the beer is wonderful!"

Joseph worked hard at his studies. He had to catch up for all those years when he had been tending cows and building sheds. He was not a very fast learner, but he made up for that by long hours of study.

When vacation time came, he would go up to Louvain to visit Auguste, now a student for the priesthood at the seminary of the Fathers of the Sacred Hearts. Auguste helped Joseph with his French.

Autumn came, bringing a touch of sadness to the countryside. The mellow colors of poplar, willow, and oak leaves were misty in the distance around Braine-le-

Comte. And, in the mind of Joseph de Veuster, a big question waited to be answered. He had been wondering more and more if he were really cut out for a business career. Often, at night, while the others were in their beds, he would kneel in his room praying, trying to decide what to do.

In October, the Redemptorist Fathers gave a mission at their beautiful church in Braine-le-Comte. Father Joseph was an eloquent preacher.

"Foolish sinner," he cried, "who for a fleeting moment of pleasure condemns himself to an eternity of pain!"

The priest's fiery words rang in Joseph's ears as he walked back with his companions through the dark streets to the school. As the boys talked about the sermon, they hardly noticed that Joseph walked beside them without speaking. He was often that way. Not for nothing had they given him the nickname "Silent Joseph".

That night he lay awake and thought. Now he felt certain God was calling him to the religious life. But what would his father say? What would happen to the grain business? Many questions must be answered. Joseph was sure of only one thing. God wished him to become a priest!

It was not long before his chance came to bring up the touchy subject at home. His parents wrote him a letter with the good news that his sister Pauline had gone to join the Ursuline Sisters in Holland.

He sat at his desk and wrote his answer.

"How happy Pauline must be!" he told his mother and father. "My turn to choose the way I should follow will, I hope, come soon. Would it be possible for me to join my brother Pamphile?" Pamphile was Auguste's name in religion.

After mailing the letter, Joseph waited anxiously. Perhaps Mr. de Veuster would be angry. At least, he would be terribly disappointed that Joseph did not want to follow his father's plans for his future. As for his mother, Joseph did not really feel she would mind. In fact, he thought his mother would be happy to have him, the fourth one of her children, enter the religious life.

But his wise parents had no intention of taking that letter too seriously! After talking the matter over with their parish priest, they took a wait-and-see attitude. Perhaps Joseph would change his mind. At any rate, they knew he had a way of becoming more and more determined if someone tried to keep him from what he wanted.

Joseph talked it over with Brother Pamphile on one of his visits to Louvain. "Why don't they answer my letter? I'm so sure I want to enter the seminary. I wish I could be a Trappist."

"The Trappist life is very strict", Pamphile put in.

"I know. Working with tools, fields, and animals. Prayer. Silence. These are all things I have learned to like."

"You could have all that right here", Pamphile argued. "Why not see if you could join our community?"

Joseph already knew something of the religious society to which his brother belonged. Pamphile told him the rest of the story.

The Congregation of the Sacred Hearts of Jesus and Mary had been started during the French Revolution—on Christmas night in the year 1800. Its founder, Father Marie-Joseph Coudrin, a young fugitive priest, had started his society in the shadow of the guillotine itself. He had been secretly ordained in Paris; his first years as a priest were filled with narrow escapes and thrilling adventure. He had even gone about in disguise at times in order to administer the sacraments to the faithful.

The violence and horror of the revolution led Father Coudrin, a hunted priest with a price on his head, to devote his life to making reparation to the Sacred Heart of Jesus. He chose to do this through perpetual adoration of the Blessed Sacrament. Out of his resolve grew the idea of his community, which started in an old house in Paris. They were sometimes called Picpus Fathers, for their first home was in Picpus Street.

The story, as Pamphile told it, caught Joseph's imagination. Besides, the Fathers of the Sacred Hearts were missionaries. He thought of that far-off day when he and Pamphile, with the others, had played at being desert fathers in the forest of Ninde.

"Father hasn't given his permission yet", Joseph said unhappily. "But I can't wait much longer. I know that's what I'm to do."

"I'll pray that he says yes—and soon!" Pamphile told his brother as he was leaving that day.

Christmas came, and Joseph could stand the family silence no longer. He must settle the question once and for all. His holiday letter home was full of strong words.

"Let me go", they said very plainly. "Let me go now!"

All his life, Joseph would find waiting very hard.

3

THE OLD TOWER FALLS

ONE WINTRY day, Mr. de Veuster stopped at the school in Braine-le-Comte. It was Joseph's nineteenth birthday, January 3, 1859, but his father's visit was unexpected.

"Get your things, Joseph", Mr. de Veuster said in his brusque way. "I've some business to do in Louvain, and you can come along and visit your brother."

Joseph was always glad of a chance to talk to Pamphile.

On the train to Louvain, Mr. de Veuster was silent. He took out his ruled ledger and busied himself with grain prices and profits. Joseph sat across from him uneasily, wishing his father would bring up the subject of his future, but hardly daring to speak of it himself.

"Here we are, Joseph." The train had pulled into the station at Louvain. They went out into the city square in the pale wintry sunlight.

"You go see Pamphile for a while. I'll be busy around the market for several hours, and, when I've finished my business for the day, I'll stop and pick you up."

Mr. de Veuster straightened his heavy coat with a quick gesture and started off in one direction. Joseph, puzzled and thoughtful, set off in the other.

Brother Pamphile greeted Joseph warmly. As it was a special day, Joseph's birthday, Pamphile had been given permission for a long visit. They exchanged family news. Louvain was only a few miles from Tremeloo, and Pamphile could visit at home quite often.

"And what about you?" Pamphile asked. "Has Father said anything yet?"

"Nothing." Joseph shook his head. "But I can't wait any longer. God is calling me, and I must obey."

"Why don't you speak to our superior, Father Wincke, this afternoon? I've already told him you would like to enter the congregation."

Joseph hesitated. "I don't suppose it would do any harm to have a talk with him", he said doubtfully.

"Come on, then", Pamphile urged. "We'll stop in the chapel for a visit on the way."

Father Wenceslas Wincke looked across his wide desk and smiled encouragingly at the young man before him. A good judge of character, Father Wincke now studied Joseph de Veuster carefully. He saw a typical Flemish farm boy, with somewhat rough manners and an awkward way of speaking.

"I've come to ask you to accept me as a postulant in the Congregation of the Fathers of the Sacred Hearts", Joseph had blurted out.

"I know", replied the superior. "Your brother has spoken to me about your desire to enter the religious life."

As Father Wenceslas questioned Joseph kindly on his motives and qualifications, he could not help noticing the sincerity and straightforwardness of the young man. And there could be no doubt that he was blessed with good health and more than average strength, both needed for the hard work and discipline of the Picpus Fathers.

"Perhaps your vocation is to be with us, my son," said the wise priest, "but I do not think we could accept you as a student for the priesthood. You know, of course, that you haven't had the schooling needed for seminary studies."

Joseph realized this only too well. It was a keen disappointment, though, that his dream of becoming a priest could never come to pass.

"—but as a brother in our community," Father was saying, "I think you would be able to find your place or, rather, God's place for you."

Joseph accepted the superior's decision humbly. Whether he became a priest or not—whatever he did— was in God's hands.

"When would you be ready to come?" Father Wenceslas asked.

"Why—right now—today!" Joseph stopped quickly, and his face reddened as he realized how hurriedly he had spoken.

Father Wenceslas smiled and, standing up, extended his hand to Joseph.

"I understand your impatience, my son", he told the young Fleming. "But first you must speak to your father. If he agrees, then you may stay with us today."

Joseph stayed for dinner as the guest of Brother Pamphile. In the early evening, Mr. de Veuster knocked at the monastery door. Joseph and Pamphile were waiting for him.

After a brief greeting, Mr. de Veuster turned to go.

"Where's your coat, Joseph?" he asked.

"Father—I'm not going back with you."

Mr. de Veuster looked sharply at Joseph.

"Not going, Son?"

"No, Father. I talked to Father Wenceslas. He says that, with your permission, I may stay and become a postulant."

Mr. de Veuster buttoned his dark coat and turned up the collar. It was a bitter cold night.

"Well, then, if that's the case, I'll be going along to get my train." No anger. No surprise, even. Mr. de Veuster was not a man for sentiment, but Joseph saw that his father was struggling to be composed.

Suddenly, Joseph took his father's arm.

"I'll go with you to the station, Father", he said.

"That will be fine, Joseph, fine." The two set out in silence. Perhaps, Joseph thought, this was the very reason his father had brought him to Louvain this day. But he was never to know for certain whether Mr. de Veuster had planned things to turn out exactly this way!

After the train had left for Tremeloo, Joseph turned back alone. His heavy shoes clomped down Bondgenootenlaan Street and Mansche Street and, finally, down the very narrow cobbled street in Mount Saint Anthony, where the house of the Fathers of the Sacred Hearts stood.

He had forgotten his coat, but he did not notice the cold. With his huge strides, he passed by the many-windowed houses, looking for all the world like an athlete off for a title match on some playing field. And indeed he was! For, just as he entered the gate of the monastery, the bell for night prayers was ringing, and he hurried to the chapel to kneel with the others and ask God's blessing on his new life.

Joseph fell easily into the routine of life at Louvain. There was never any lack of jobs for one so strong and willing as he was. For his name in religion he chose

Damien, after the heroic doctor martyred when the Church was young.

When the work began on the new chapel, Brother Damien was quickly assigned to the building crew.

"Over here, Brother Damien. Dump them right here!" The load of bricks was laid next to the masonry wall that was going up, and Damien stood up straight and mopped his sweating face with his big handkerchief. Then he started back with his wheelbarrow for another load.

"Wait. Hold on, there. Don't bring any more just yet!" one of the workmen called to him. "We've got to solve a problem here first."

"A problem?"

"Yes, see that old chimney tower over there?" Damien looked and nodded.

"It has to go before we can get on with the chapel. It's in the way. We need to figure out how to get rid of it."

Damien studied the tower. He walked over and went around it. The masonry that had once held the bricks together was crumbled. The bricks stood one upon the other only out of habit, or in plain defiance of the laws of gravity.

"They couldn't blast it", he observed. "Too close to the other buildings. Somebody has to climb up and take it down brick by brick."

"Who wants to risk his neck doing that?" another lay brother put in. "The whole thing might fall from the weight of the ladder."

The foreman of the building job came over. "That's all for today, men", he told them. "We'll try to find someone willing to tackle that tower."

"Let me try it", Damien spoke up. Impulsively, he stepped forward and seized a nearby ladder.

The rest quickly gathered around to watch.

"Is Brother Damien going to try it?"

"How can he possibly make it?"

Damien steadied the ladder and put his foot firmly on the lowest rung. Slowly, he took a few steps upward. The ladder quivered beneath Damien's weight. But he continued his slow upward climb.

Up he went to the very top. Now he could reach the uppermost loose brick. He took it off the edge, and a shower of powdery masonry fell on his head. He did not stop to brush it off but continued down until he could hand the brick to one of the men below. Then back up again for another, over and over. The ladder creaked and seemed to sway, but his step was steady. At last, he brought the tower down to a height where the other workmen could easily get at it. When he stepped down from the ladder, a small cheer went up from the bystanders.

"Good for you, Brother Damien. Good for you!"

But Damien was busy shaking the dust from his hair and clothing. He would just have time to get washed and into his habit before dinner.

One day, Father Verhaege, who was in charge of the seminarians, called Damien to his room.

"I hear you've been learning some Latin, Brother." Father Verhaege did not smile, and Damien was slightly ill at ease. Was the priest displeased with him? Maybe Father thought that learning Latin was a bit too ambitious for a lay brother.

"That's right, Father Verhaege", Damien answered. "It's—well, it started as a game between Brother Pamphile and me. During recreation, or while he studies, he sometimes goes over some Latin with me."

"I see. Do you like this game?" asked Father Verhaege.

"Yes, very much. You see, Father, I haven't had much schooling. I'd like to make up for what I've missed along that line."

"Brother Pamphile tells me you are a very good pupil indeed. I have given him permission to go ahead with your lessons—this time seriously, not just as a game."

"Thank you, Father Verhaege. I'll be grateful for the chance to learn."

Father moved with Damien toward the door of his study.

"You are adapting yourself well to our way of life, Brother Damien", he told him. "I believe you can become a good religious, with God's help, and if you try hard. You know your failings—that temper of yours and those occasional sharp words. You can overcome these, but it isn't going to be easy. Patience, Brother Damien, is one thing I hope you'll learn from our life here."

"I know. I'm in too much of a hurry. I've always been that way. But I'm going to try even harder to improve."

Father Verhaege smiled. "Sometimes it's good to be in a hurry. That can be a sign of generosity or even of heroism. But here we all have to control our impatience."

Damien knew his temper sometimes got the better of him. His quick Flemish tongue could lash out in momentary anger, although afterward he would be full of remorse and rush to apologize to the injured one.

Now he worked harder than ever at his Latin, begging Pamphile to spend every spare moment teaching him.

The next time Father Verhaege called Damien to his office, he handed the young man a Latin book used by the fifth-year students.

"Here, Brother Damien, see what you can do with this."

Damien took the book and began to read from it quickly, without stumbling.

"I see you've really mastered this." Father Verhaege was clearly satisfied with the young novice's progress. "We've decided to let you join the class of seminarians. Oh, it's just on a trial basis. See what you can do."

Damien's heart was beating excitedly. So he might become a priest after all! He tried to tell Father Verhaege how happy he was, but, as usual, he just didn't have the right words. Instead, he went straight to the chapel. There his awkward speech did not get in his way. God knew what he meant! God understood his gratitude!

Here, before the Blessed Sacrament, Damien spent the best moments of each day. In keeping with the inspiration of Father Coudrin, their founder, every day each member of the Congregation of the Sacred Hearts spent half an hour, and weekly one hour at night, watching before the Blessed Sacrament. This perpetual adoration was a never-ending act of reparation for the sins of the world.

Damien, because of his unusual physical strength and his willingness to do hard things, had been given the hour from two to three in the morning. His strong body had learned to accept the loss of sleep, the hard kneeling bench, the chilly chapel. His strong will chose the difficult way. While the others slept, Damien would pray in the silent chapel, asking for grace to meet the challenge of his tremendous calling.

Often, in the still pastures near his home, he had prayed in a peace very much like this. He, more than the other de Veuster boys, had liked the job of sheeptending. He had never found it boring because it had given him time to pray and meditate.

Now, the first step toward his great ideal was at hand! It happened on an October day at the motherhouse at Issy, just outside Paris, where Damien had gone to prepare for his religious profession.

The choir was singing: "Let us go to the house of the Lord . . ." Brother Damien, carrying his lighted candle, entered the chapel with the other novices.

Placing his hands in the hands of the priest at the altar, Damien took the three vows of poverty, chastity, and obedience. He gave his solemn promise to live and die as a member of the Congregation of the Sacred Hearts of Jesus and Mary. Then, as Damien and the other newly professed men prostrated themselves before the altar, the celebrating priest sang: "Have mercy on me, O God! Have mercy on me!" Four priests held the large black cloth, symbolic of the funeral pall, over Damien. The candles cast their glow, light as a breath. Death to the world, now and forever!

It was over quickly, but the scene was burned into Damien's memory as if it had been a picture drawn with fire! There was one more thing. The newly professed must seal the promise with his signature.

"Damien de Veuster—" It was written so firmly in his heavy hand that we can still read it on the page. When he laid down the pen, Damien had signed away his life. He knew it, and he meant it. Just what that renunciation was to mean he did not yet know. But he had begun to dream already of distant mission lands.

On Easter Sunday, the Picpus Fathers of Issy had a noted visitor—Tepano Jaussen, great missionary of the society and bishop of Tahiti for thirteen years. As Bishop Jaussen celebrated a solemn pontifical Mass in the monastery chapel, Damien counted more than twenty priests at the altar. Uniformed French soldiers added their voices to the joyful singing of the congregation.

Later, Bishop Jaussen spoke to the students about his missionary travels. "A land of unbelievable natural beauty"—the Pacific islands called Oceania.

"Our society is still young; yet it has already begun to answer the challenge in the South Seas." He told them about Hawaii, the Sacred Hearts Fathers' first mission field, which they had been given in 1825. Later, their apostolate had widened to include other islands—the Gambier, the Marquesas.

Bishop Jaussen spoke glowingly of the wonders of the South Seas and of his own life there as a missionary. As Damien listened, his generous heart seemed to be on fire. If only he, too, could go there! Sitting there in the quiet chapel, he felt those distant islands calling him.

"There lies the field," Bishop Jaussen told them passionately, "white for the harvest—the harvest of your missionary labors!"

Strange! This farm boy, who had known only the placid waterways of Flanders or, perhaps, had seen how the tides of the distant North Sea could suddenly send the water climbing around the mossy piles on Malines wharves, now saw himself, crucifix in hand, standing upon the shores of Oceania. A glorious vision.

Rumors flew through the monastery that Bishop Jaussen on his return would take some of the men from Issy with him. But Damien dared not hope he would be one of them, for he was not yet an ordained priest.

No, his time had not yet come! Back he went to Louvain to spend another year studying advanced theology and philosophy at the university. As he tramped in and out of the historic halls that had seen so many noted scholars come and go for hundreds of years, Damien gripped his notebook tightly and wished he could be as brilliant as some of his fellow students. He took notes furiously. Every night he bent over his study desk, trying to absorb every thought, every idea.

Sometimes he carried his zeal a little too far. Father Wenceslas noticed one day that Damien's desk had a motto on it. It was an excellent motto: "Silence, Prayer, Recollection!" The only trouble was that Damien had carved it with his knife into the top of his wooden desk! That brought a scolding—before all the other students, too.

But if Damien sometimes went too far, it was all a part of his eagerness to do more, to do better. Pamphile had often wakened at night to find his brother's bed untouched and Damien sleeping on the floor. Then, too, he had the habit of eating always at the second table in the refectory, where meat shortages often occurred. Damien would slip his portion to the next man, unnoticed, and make his own meal of vegetables. A big sacrifice for a husky fellow with a naturally huge appetite!

It seemed certain that Pamphile's chance to work in foreign fields would come first, for he was now ordained. One day in July of 1863, Father Pamphile rushed into the room the brothers shared.

"Listen to this, Damien. I have my orders. Bishop Maigret, vicar apostolic of the Hawaiian Islands, has asked for a group of missionaries. I am to sail for Honolulu in October!"

4

CALL TO THE SOUTH SEAS

THE BELLS of Louvain tolled often that summer of
1863.

The bells of Saint Peter's, the city's main church, with
its lovely fifteenth-century Gothic spire; the bells of
Saint Michael's, in their elaborately carved baroque
stonework; the bells of Saint Quentin's, ringing clear in
their straight-walled tower; the bells of Saint Gertrude's,

from their steeple graceful as a lady's dancing dress—they all tolled over the tile-roofed houses that huddled close together up and down the cobbled streets. The many tiny gables on their roofs were like so many eyes looking out on the passing of centuries.

Behind the shuttered windows now, there were tears and sorrow. The ancient Brabant capital, Belgium's citadel of learning, had stood bravely against many attacking armies in its long history. Now it was almost helpless against a new enemy—the dreaded disease of typhus. Leaving hardly a family untouched, the plague swept over the town all through the warm summer. The death carts bumped up and down the twisted streets. Before them, with the other priests of the city, hurried Father Pamphile, carrying the Last Sacraments to the bedsides of the sick. Morning, noon, and night, without thinking of the danger to himself, he kept up his visits, hardly stopping to sleep or to eat his meals.

The summer finally dragged into autumn, and in the Picpus House in Mount Saint Anthony the bags were piling up—clothes, medicines, altar vessels. Pamphile and the others were trying to gather their supplies for the mission journey. Damien helped all he could. His own heart was heavy because it was not he who was going, but he tried to hide his feelings.

One day, early in October, a few weeks before the sailing, Pamphile hurried home in a dry wind, his eyes too bright, his face too hot, a nagging ache in every bone of his tired body.

The next day, and for a long time after that, he lay in bed, a victim of the disease he had so bravely challenged. Father Wenceslas felt the young priest's burning forehead and turned gravely to Damien.

"His life is in God's hands. This may last another week. And, even if he lives, he won't be able to make the voyage. I must write Father General to cancel his passage."

Poor Pamphile! In his delirium he talked of Hawaii and sometimes imagined himself tossed about in a wild storm at sea. When his mind cleared for a few minutes, he would turn to Damien with tortured eyes.

It was worse to be awake and to know that his dream of being a foreign missionary was, for the time being at least, shattered.

Damien, watching night and day in the quiet room, saw a door swinging open for him just as it was swinging shut for his sick brother. Rather than let the ticket be wasted, for it had already been bought from the shipping company, why shouldn't he, Damien, take Pamphile's place? A wonderful idea! He glanced at the suitcases neatly piled in the corner of the room.

"How about it, Pamphile? I'll go instead of you. Then you can rest easy and get better fast. You'll be sent out to the islands with the next group to sail!"

"If only you could go," Pamphile answered weakly, "but Father Wenceslas would never let you. You're not even through your studies yet, and you'd have to be ordained before he would send you to the missions." All the same, a faint gleam of hope brightened the sick man's eyes for the first time.

"Oh, but this is a special case", Damien argued. "I know what I'll do! I won't even ask Father Wenceslas. I'll write to the Father General of our congregation in the motherhouse in Paris!"

"That's a daring thing to do, Damien."

"Never mind, I have to do it." Damien was up in a flash, grabbing pen and paper. He began to write furiously fast. The words fell over one another on the sheet, and a few ink blots appeared here and there. Damien couldn't stop to worry over neatness or spelling. He sent the letter off at once, making sure Father Wenceslas knew nothing about his plan.

Long days of waiting and worry followed. The time for the sailing drew nearer. What if the answer was no? Even worse, what if Father General was offended at the young seminarian's boldness in writing to him directly? Maybe Damien would get a good scolding when Father Wenceslas heard about his scheme.

The only thing that really mattered to him was that he should be allowed to go!

In the motherhouse of the Sacred Hearts Fathers in Paris, the Father General tore open Damien's hastily written plea. He glanced first at the name. Damien de Veuster—but who was he? One of the students at the Louvain house, evidently. Oh, yes, he remembered now. The awkward youth from Tremeloo. Why on earth should Damien de Veuster be writing to him?

Almost every day, now, letters were coming to the Father General, as head of a missionary order, asking for priests and brothers for far-off lands. There was a never-ending plea for more missionaries. Of course, Father General thought, it was worse than useless to send out someone so young, inexperienced, and evidently so rash as this Damien appeared to be. Still—the priest's hand absently spun the huge globe on his desk. A world was waiting!

He rose quickly and called his secretary. Tossing him the letter, he said: "Here, write back and tell him it's all right with me. He can go."

That was how Damien, sitting at the table in the refectory at Louvain, received his answer. It was handed to him or, rather, thrown at him, by a momentarily annoyed Father Wenceslas, who thought the whole idea pretty wild.

"Don't you think you're rushing things a bit, wanting to run off to the missions so early?" Father Wenceslas spoke coldly.

Damien heard the harshness of the older man's voice, but it hardly touched him. Instead, his eyes devoured the words of the brief note. It said he could go! That was all he wanted. Forgetting to eat the meal that was in front of him, he jumped up and rushed to Pamphile's room, waving the miraculous letter in the air.

"I can go, Pamphile! I can go!"

"Thank the good Lord!" Pamphile answered simply, and lay back on his pillows.

Then Damien was off to the de Veuster farmhouse to say good-bye to his family. His long steps shortened the miles between Louvain and Tremeloo almost without his noticing it. He burst into the kitchen, and there, for the first time, he felt a sharp thrust of painful memory as he looked around the familiar room.

All at once he remembered the hours spent there reading from the old saints' book, the copper pots giving back the cheery glow of the firelight, just as they did today. And in the corner, unchanged through all the years of his growing up, the crucifix still hung against the wall.

Triumphantly, he broke the news of his going. Mrs. de Veuster, who had never expected such a thing to happen to him so soon, busied herself more than usual about the preparation of the evening meal. She did not trust herself to look up too often at her youngest son. Not that she rebelled at the life he had chosen that was taking him from her forever! She was proud to have a missionary son, but, still, it was hard to let him go.

At the dinner table, with all the family gathered around, Damien talked excitedly of his future. Buried deep inside him was the thought that he would not see these dear faces again. When it was time to go back to Louvain, he still couldn't bear to say good-bye to his mother.

"Meet me tomorrow morning at Our Lady of Montaigu", he whispered to her, as the others bade him their parting wishes.

She nodded silently. It was a place they both loved.

Every year Damien had made the pilgrimage to this famous Flemish shrine of our Blessed Mother at Montaigu, near the town of Diest. With the other seminarians, he had risen at midnight and set out in the darkness, like pilgrims of olden times. They would walk until dawn, arriving at the church just in time for the early Mass.

This night Damien walked alone. His firm step on the silent roads took him northward, and when the faint light of dawn came, the majestic dome of the church drew itself up on its high hilltop in the distance.

Looking down the empty road that stretched toward Tremeloo, he saw his mother, a lonely figure in the gray light. That must be his sister-in-law, Marie, walking beside her. They met but did not speak.

Inside, the six o'clock Mass was just beginning. The big votive candles lighted the ancient statue of the Mother of Sorrows. They were lit year after year by countless pilgrims bringing their special prayers to our Lady's feet. Sheaves of abandoned crutches surrounded her time-worn figure, the harvest of faith already reaped by some who had walked away from her shrine unaided.

After Mass, the silence of the little group that stayed to pray a while was broken only by the occasional sound of Mrs. de Veuster's well-used rosary beads. They prayed for each other—the mother for the son, the son for the mother—for the trials each must face.

When they came out at last, the business of the day

was beginning around them. The carts rolled along the stone street to the market in town with fresh fruits and vegetables from neighboring farms.

Damien lingered behind, looking over his shoulder and quickly drawing his handkerchief from the folds of his cassock.

His mother turned.

"Why so slow, Jef?" she asked in a low voice.

"One last look, Mother. I'll never see Our Lady of Montaigu again." At that moment, Hawaii was a world and more away from everything he loved!

"I prayed that I might have twelve years in the missions", he told her. "Twelve years to work for Christ—that's all I ask."

They stood, somewhat uncertain. This was the moment of parting, but how could they make it pass with least pain?

Just then a loud clatter broke out on the cobblestones, and Damien, turning, saw the carriage for Louvain coming along. The driver, mistaking Damien's glance for a summons and noticing his cassock, thought he must want a ride, so he reined his horses sharply and drew to a noisy stop.

Damien stepped aside and mounted the carriage suddenly. He looked back only once as they drove off. Marie, he saw, had taken his mother's arm as they turned back to the old familiar road to Ninde. They could not speak to each other, so they said the Rosary all the way back to the farmhouse.

Damien, though, had little time for reflection. Things were happening too fast. He had to hurry to Paris to be in time for the special retreat for the missionaries.

Father General himself was preaching this retreat. He had thought out very carefully what to say to these men. He wanted to prepare them well for the hardships they would surely meet. Now, as he stood before them in the quiet chapel, he spoke earnestly. His keen eyes rested first on one face and then another. He tried to measure the man behind each one!

Father Chrétien Willemsen—a man of sound judgment. In fact, Father General felt very safe in putting him in charge of the whole group. Brother Clement and Brother Lievin, missionary brothers—they would be needed in getting the mission stations set up in that wild outpost to which they were going.

Father General's glance came to rest on an unfamiliar face. Oh, it must be Damien de Veuster! The prelate went on speaking in his even voice about the spiritual dangers of the missionary life, but his eyes stayed on the broad, good-natured face of the young student. Twenty-three, he would guess, surely no more! A picture of robust health and straightforward courage. Why, he looked positively boyish under his shock of thick dark hair. And the shoulders under the plain cassock reminded Father General of those powerful Brabantine workhorses that were also Flemish, like Damien.

So this was the writer of that impetuous letter! Was I wrong to let him go, Damien's father-in-religion was asking himself? This was no time to send a boy on a man's errand. The Hawaiian missions—there, if ever—a man of great endurance, great faith, was needed!

The conference was ended. Father General turned to kneel on the altar step. There was a shuffling of feet as the retreatants shifted position behind him.

No, he did not think he had made a mistake. Something in this young man's face told the Father General he had been right after all. He began to pray:

"Almighty and eternal God . . . direct your servants along the way of eternal salvation. May their life be hidden in Christ, so that, with your help, they may not only desire the things that are pleasing to you but, with all their strength, may do them . . ."

There was time for Damien to do just one more thing. He had his photograph taken to send home. It showed him standing very straight in his black cassock, holding the large crucifix. His steady eyes had grown a little nearsighted, but the firm gaze was the same under the wide brow. The picture was a little too posed, but still a good likeness of him—a sort of farewell gift to Tremeloo. He inscribed it and sent it off by post.

After that, there was just time to gather up all the assorted pieces of strapped or string-tied luggage and rush off to the railroad station. The whole mission party, one father, five brothers of the Sacred Hearts, and some Sacred Hearts sisters, who were also sailing, met at East Station in Paris, at nine o'clock in the morning, on October 29. It seemed, surrounded by a sea of baggage as they were, that they had supplies enough for the rest of their lives.

It was a long journey aboard the Paris-Cologne-Hamburg Express. The day passed, and, when night fell, Damien stared out of the window as the train whistled, puffed, and streaked over the dark and unfamiliar countryside. One by one, the tired father and brothers dozed, their knees wedged uncomfortably between suitcases. But Damien did not sleep. It was a habit of his to watch and pray at night. This night, above all, as not for resting. Each moment the humming wheels brought him nearer to his destination. All his prayers were about to be answered. He was excited and happier than he had ever been before.

At noon on Friday, the roofs of the old port of Bremerhaven came into sight. The missionaries stretched their stiff muscles and made for the wharves, where their ship was waiting, flying, in the fresh harbor breeze, the colorful red, white, and blue flag of Hawaii.

5

VOYAGE ROUND THE HORN

D AMIEN, in his broad-brimmed black hat and flowing soutane, stood on the afterdeck of the merchant ship *R. M. Wood*.

The fast-moving vessel drew farther and farther away
from the bustling wharves of Bremerhaven. Damien
watched the waters fan out sharply and the fading coast-
line grow smaller and smaller. A mild wind in the harbor

had freshened into a stiff breeze, bellying out the huge sails over his head.

The excitement of travel and homesickness for Tremeloo blended with the exaltation of Damien's mood. In the retreat just ended back in Paris, the Father General had urged the missionaries fervently on their high adventure, the saving of souls. It seemed to Damien now that no one had ever set out on a more thrilling quest.

Later, in his somewhat cramped cabin, he sat down to write his thoughts to his family. A few minutes before, as Bremerhaven had swung beneath the horizon, he had looked upon the shores of Europe for the last time.

"The graces of our state are so powerful that the greatest difficulties and trials do not trouble us", he wrote. This was the first of many such letters, full of flashing courage.

Back in quiet Tremeloo, the River Dyle would soon be freezing over, ringing with the wild shouts of boys and girls and the sound of skates on glistening ice. Across the broad, flat fields, the first snow would fly, clouding the bare wooden arms of the windmills against the gray winter sky. The bells of Saint Rombaut would peal louder and clearer in the frosty air.

Damien made his way to the ship's helm and felt the spray on his face. He turned to see Captain Geerken standing beside him. This rugged captain had already piloted his ship seven times to Honolulu and back.

"The great adventure's beginning, Brother Damien.

Five months of this and we should see the volcanoes of Hawaii. Have you ever seen a volcano?"

"No," said Damien, "but I think they will be powerful reminders of the power of God, Captain."

"Hawaii is a paradise. You're lucky to be going to it."

"I hope to lead souls there to an even better paradise", Damien said simply.

Now the ship's bell was the ruler of the long days. The six missionaries planned their daily life as nearly as they could to follow their usual rule. Hours for work, study, sleep, and recreation were the same as at Louvain. The only priest among them, Father Chrétien, acted as superior. He celebrated Holy Mass each morning on the portable altar Damien set up in the ship's dining hall.

Sometimes Damien found his job as sacristan could be quite difficult, especially when the rolling sea threatened to overturn the altar at any moment. Ten sisters of the Sacred Hearts were making the voyage on the *Wood*. Their superior had returned to Louvain after seeing them off.

"Your brother is another Aloysius Gonzaga", she told Pamphile, enthusiastically. "You couldn't hear Mass when he was serving without being struck by his devotion."

Soon most of the missionaries were seasick and had to stay below in their narrow cabins with the none too comfortable double-decker bunks. Damien, following Captain Geerken's expert advice, soon got his sea legs. Father Chrétien, who suffered more than any of the others during the voyage, was glad he had this strong

Flemish farm boy to take over the duties of all the others from time to time.

"Damien has really been the man of the hour", Father Chrétien wrote painfully in his diary. "One morning, when the sea was particularly rough, I didn't even have the courage to start Mass, but Damien's firm will urged me on. He keeps up all our spirits."

Damien even acted as infirmarian, prescribing simple remedies for the discomforts of the others and waiting on them when they were confined to their bunks.

"We have no more hosts", Father Chrétien said to him one day. "What can we do, Brother Damien?"

Damien went straight to the ship's steward for help. The steward gave him some flour, and Damien, the sleeves of his cassock rolled up above his elbows, was soon busy trying to find some way to make a new supply of hosts for Mass. The first experiment did not turn out very well. He tried again. After several failures, he managed to produce a usable host. By that time, there was quite a bit of flour around the galley, and the smell of salt pork in barrels secured in the passageway nearby was getting to be a little too much even for Damien's strong stomach!

Sleeping in the tiny cabins was not easy for a big fellow like Damien. There was little room to stretch his powerful muscles. Besides, he loved the silence of the night watches on deck, where one could think and pray uninterrupted. He began helping the crew with their work. They, in turn, were at first amused and then impressed by his skill. He quickly learned to scale the masts and manage the vast overhead network of ropes and sails. He knew their names like an old sailor. Without the slightest fear of falling, he would tuck up his cassock and climb to the topmost sail, leaning confidently into the wind as he untangled and knotted the heavy ropes.

Captain Geerken guided his vessel with a sure hand, south and still south, crossing parallel after parallel that brought the equator ever closer.

They had now left winter behind. The sun beat down, pleasantly warm at first, then baking hot. The cabins were stifling, and the ever-present smell of beans and pork turned the travelers quite away from the idea of eating.

Then the wind died down, and a strange calm came over the water. There was nothing in the world but slow water, slow ship, and the ever-present sun!

"Want to see the equator, Brother Damien?" Captain Geerken, a hearty smile on his weathered face, was holding out his binoculars. Damien put the glass to his eyes and peered southward. Sure enough, there was the equator, a dark line cutting the circle of sea in two. Damien looked again!

Captain Geerken began to roar with laughter.

"See it?" he shouted.

Damien turned the glasses around and looked closely at the lens. So that was Captain Geerken's equator, a hair carefully pasted across the glass! It was a good joke. Damien wanted to try it on his companions.

"When do we actually cross the equator—the real one, I mean?" Damien asked.

"Early tomorrow", Captain Geerken answered. "I hope you're ready for a visit from old King Neptune himself! He always comes aboard to demand his due."

Damien had heard of the sailors' age-old custom of paying forfeit to the king of the deep whenever a ship crossed the equator. Still, he was a bit surprised the next morning when the old king, looking very fierce indeed with whiskers and trident, actually appeared on deck! The *R. M. Wood* took on a holiday air as everyone in turn had to pay his penalty. Sometimes those forfeits were rather rough and resulted in a good drenching for the poor victim. Damien and the other missionaries paid their forfeit—two bottles of wine apiece. This pleased the sailors, and everyone pretended not to notice that the boatswain was missing so long as King Neptune remained on board.

At night, when all was quiet, Damien liked to be on deck. He loved the mystery of the sea and its brooding calm. The slow calls of the watch were solemn, like responses in some religious ceremony.

Most of all, Damien loved the silence. He was in tune with the men of the sea and could enjoy their chanteys shouted in rough tones. But, most of all, he could enjoy their peace in the dark hours when the stars seemed made just for them, reflecting God's majesty, and men made patient by the ways of wind and water could dream.

He himself was growing impatient! He longed to leap over those thousands of miles of water. He sometimes felt like a man standing still and waiting for his journey's end to come to him. Somewhere off there, slowly creeping toward him, was Hawaii, with those unknown souls whose salvation was now his life.

On New Year's Day, 1864, they were twenty-two degrees below the equator. Damien watched the crew fishing for strange creatures that played in the calm tropical waters—sharks and huge porpoises, weighing several hundred pounds.

Toward the middle of January, they neared Cape Horn. The air had grown colder and colder, and the winds blew harsh. The waters that had lain peacefully around them now leaped like dragons, with white teeth of foam gnashing the stripped decks.

There were no more pleasant strolls with the captain or thrilling trips aloft for Damien.

"The Horn has its own tricks", Captain Geerken said darkly. He had rounded it often enough to know. And there were tales he had heard from fellow sea captains—terrible stories of men being swept overboard and swallowed by the waves. He ordered everything movable tied down securely and had the crew prepare for a quick rescue operation.

But the winds were still rising. Men made fast the furled sails with hurrying hands. The *Wood* seemed to hang on cliffs of water.

Captain Geerken, swathed in oilskins, strode up and

down, his sextant searching for a break in the threatening skies.

Below decks, Father Chrétien and his little band huddled in the damp and drafty dining hall.

"Remember the *Marie-Joseph* . . ."

The story was in the thoughts of all of them. Damien had heard it told often enough back home in the novitiate—how a storm had swallowed that ill-fated ship in this very spot some twenty years before, taking with her twenty-five missionaries of the Sacred Hearts. Now each one of them asked himself: "How would I face this kind of martyrdom?"

They knew it was possible that this tragic drama might be played again. All around them wreckage floated, silently telling its grim tale.

For days now, the *Wood* had been at the mercy of the sea, driven much farther south than her course lay.

Then Damien had to give up trying to secure the altar for Mass these mornings. The men could hardly stand upright, much less the chalice!

"We'll begin a special novena", Father Chrétien told them. Each day they prayed. On the last day, the Feast of the Purification, the wind fell, and the black waters seemed to be smoothed by a giant hand.

Captain Geerken shouted with relief. "We're safe now", he exclaimed. "We'll make it all right."

"Of course", Damien answered with a smile. "We just finished our novena."

Gradually they were able to swing the ship around and

head her back again, this time to the north. Now they would sail up from the bottom of the world, off the west shore of South America. Straight toward Hawaii the winds now carried them, the sails drying fast as they sped along. Everyone's clothes were beginning to dry out, too. Things on board were so wet it took a few days of bright sunlight to warm away the smell of wetness and staleness everywhere.

Seven thousand more miles to go—and another great storm to be weathered. This time it came at night. The ship shot perilously up the angry swells like a paper boat.

Captain Geerken was on deck shouting orders to his crew. He was afraid the mast might snap before they managed to haul the sails in. This time the helmsmen were lashed to their posts so they would not be washed over the side. Meditation was pretty hard, even for Damien, amid the crashing of millions of tons of mad water. But Damien stood his ground. He could even tell a funny story to lighten the long hours of anxious waiting out the storm.

Coming as he did from the farming land of Flanders, it was strange he felt so native to the sea. For one thing, he had the stamina to endure the hardships of a long sea voyage. And he had, above all, an unshaken faith that he would arrive safely. Hadn't he put his hopes into the gentle hands of Our Lady at Montaigu?

Once again, the ship rode out the danger and soon fell easily into Magellan's course, driven northward by the same trade winds, navigating the same waters. They passed the Juan Fernandez Islands, made famous by the shipwreck of Robinson Crusoe.

"And over there," Captain Geerken pointed to a distant speck of land one clear morning, "that's Pitcairn Island, where the descendants of the *Bounty* mutineers still live."

There was Easter Island, too, whose mysteries no one yet had fully explored, and the peaceful Marquesas. The sea stretched out, beautiful and peaceful, around them, and the sky smiled day after day, as if incapable of ill temper. Damien again found hours for night walking and praying.

When they came again to the equator, they were under full sail and bearing rapidly on, past the coasts of Panama, Costa Rica, and Guatemala.

On March 17, after five months at sea, the lookout gave the cry everyone had awaited so long.

"Land ahead!" Such excitement! Sleep was forgotten. Everyone crowded the forward deck, watching the Hawaiian Islands grow from dark blobs on the horizon into steep cliffs rising majestically above coasts of tropical splendor.

"There it is." Captain Geerken pointed his blunt finger. "Your first volcano, Father Damien. Take a good look. You'll be seeing a lot of them!"

Damien had spent his boyhood in a land that had no mountains. Now he looked wonderingly at the distant heights rising so sharply from the sapphire water. Their tops were wrapped in a mantel of snow, though their insides burned with red-hot fire, which at times spilled forth from huge, hidden craters.

They had to pass some of the twelve islands making up the Hawaiian group before reaching their harbor. Captain Geerken pointed them out, naming the others, which they did not see as well.

Oahu, Maui, Hawaii—names strangely musical to Damien's Flemish ear. Molokai—Damien repeated it slowly.

Toward evening, on the Feast of Saint Joseph, March 19, Captain Geerken finally steered the *Wood* past the last barrier, the promontory known as Diamond Head. There lay Honolulu harbor, with open arms to welcome them!

6

LAND OF VOLCANOES

"G loria *in excelsis Deo . . .*"

The strong, vibrant voice, with its strange accent, rang out from the flower-decked altar. The Cathedral of Our Lady of Peace in Honolulu had never looked lovelier.

The face of the new priest, as he turned to the congregation, was radiantly happy. Never had a Solemn High Mass seemed more beautiful, more meaningful!

When the celebrant turned to distribute Holy Communion, hundreds of colorfully dressed, brown-skinned people came crowding to the altar rail.

Afterward, outside the cathedral, they stood respectfully, awaiting the new priest's blessing, as precious to those Hawaiian Christians as to Christians the world over.

"Your blessing, Kamiano!" Their soft voices blended into one continual murmur, as Father Damien lifted his hand again and again. He smiled, for already they seemed like his children. He knew he would like these gentle people, with their musical voices and friendly ways. But, as soon as he could, he slipped away from the crowd.

It was a solemn moment in his life, and Damien wanted above all to be alone. He was happy, gloriously happy, at the end of his first Mass. Yet, young as he was, he knew the great burden that had fallen upon his broad shoulders. He had made his dedication in this very cathedral only the day before, as Bishop Maigret placed the holy oils on his hands and bound them with the white cloth symbolic of his priestly consecration.

There was only one regret—that his parents and, particularly, his mother, had to miss this wonderful moment! He must write them this very minute.

"Do not forget, I beg you," he wrote rapidly in his excitement, "the poor priest who is going out day and night on the volcanoes of the Hawaiian Islands in search of stray sheep. Pray for me day and night. . . ."

He had hardly finished the letter when Bishop Maigret sent for him.

"You'll be assigned first to the Puna mission", the bishop told him. "That's one of the six districts of Hawaii, the largest of the Hawaiian group."

"Yes, Your Excellency. I am ready to go. When shall I leave for Puna?" Damien stood waiting for his superior's command.

Bishop Maigret, a brave missionary with many years of experience behind him, did not doubt for a moment the sincerity of the young man he had ordained the day before. But he regretted Father Damien's youth. When would they learn not to send him these raw seminarians for work that would try the wisest of priests? Still, he needed men in the mission posts so badly; he had to take what he could get.

"I've decided to take you there myself", the bishop told him. He spoke like a general who had commanded troops on many a field of battle.

"It's time for my regular visit to the Hawaiian mission. You can go along. I'll see you safely settled there, anyway." What happened afterward he would leave up to Almighty God!

"The steamer leaves early in the morning, Father Damien", the bishop said brusquely. "We can stop off at Maui Island to celebrate Mass."

Damien would have liked to stay for a while in Honolulu to learn from some of the older priests. He had, first of all, to learn a new language—one very different from his own Flemish or even the French he had mastered with so much effort.

Bishop Maigret was well known to the island people. He was greeted on all sides as he and Damien boarded the boat next day. For years they had seen him traveling tirelessly from island to island, through dangerous seas and tropical storms. Many times he had narrowly escaped death, landing on rock-ridden shores or climbing steep Hawaiian mountainsides. They knew his courage and trusted his wisdom.

At Maui, Bishop Maigret and Father Damien had just time enough to celebrate Mass in the church of the Fathers of the Sacred Hearts before they heard the steamer whistle shrilly calling them back to continue their journey. Once again, they put out to sea. Bishop Maigret did not waste time in idle conversation. He made use of the hours aboard ship to teach Damien all he could about the people, the country, and the conditions he would face at Puna.

"There are about three hundred fifty Catholics there," he explained, "and they have had no priest living among them for seven years."

Puna Mission, Damien learned, was located right on the edge of the great volcano of Kilauea, a huge mountain towering above all the others, with its huge caldera spitting fire and smoke.

"The ancient Hawaiians told many stories of Kilauea", Bishop Maigret explained. "Because they feared its eruptions so much, they believed it was the home of Pele, the pagan goddess of eternal fire. When Pele was angry, she burst forth into fire and sent burning lava down the mountainside to destroy villages and people below. The Hawaiians were terrified when this happened, and tried to please Pele with pagan rites and sacrifices . . ."

Suddenly a commotion broke out on deck behind them.

A cry went up. "Fire! Fire!" The deckhands sprang instantly into action. The fire had started in the hold, but the crew could not get to it because the passengers began to mill around in panic.

They all feared that death was threatening. Confused cries and sobs created a chaos. Bishop Maigret stepped calmly into the pushing crowd. He held up his hands for silence, and, strangely, everyone stood still and looked at him.

"Stay where you are!" Bishop Maigret's voice was the voice of one used to being in command. No one moved. He began to speak quietly, telling them that the fire would soon be brought under control by the crew. Damien stood beside him. The sight of the two priests talking to them so calmly had a wonderful effect on the fearful passengers. Soon the fire was out, but the steamer was badly damaged and had to put back into Maui harbor for repairs.

Damien was glad of this, because it gave him a little more time to spend with the fathers of his congregation at Maui. Every bit he could learn from them would be valuable at Puna.

Several days passed before another ship came by, and, meantime, Damien helped in the work of Maui

Mission. One morning he went over the mountains into the outlying countryside to celebrate Mass and hear confessions.

When he returned to the mission, he found that a boat had come by and Bishop Maigret had taken it! The vicar apostolic had no intention of slighting Damien, but his own time was far too precious to waste waiting for one new missionary. Let him find his way to Puna as best he could!

After days of hard travel by boat and on horseback, stopping occasionally at mission posts, Damien reached his destination. Part of the way he had native guides; the rest he covered alone, sometimes crawling in torn boots up steep rocky slopes and running down again into steep, plunging valleys, thick with tropical growth.

At Puna Damien found a friendly welcome waiting for him. He was the only white man in the area. There was no house for him, no church, no school. The few Catholics were widely scattered over a territory that took at least three days to cover.

"Make up your mind that the Puna mission is just beginning", Bishop Maigret had wisely warned the young priest. But Damien, as usual, was cheerful about the future.

Soon after his arrival, he was writing encouragingly to his provincial, "With energy and good conduct, these people should be excellent."

They were poor, very poor, but, as they had no desire for wealth or luxuries, this did not make them unhappy.

A little taro to eat, a straw hut with a mat on the floor, a few simple clothes—that was all they needed, or wanted. Bareheaded and barefooted, they gladly shared what they had with neighbor and stranger alike.

The Hawaiians of Puna liked the strong young missionary immediately. If he stumbled a bit sometimes over their soft-sounding Hawaiian words, they smiled. They knew he was just learning. At first, he said Mass in native huts. Then he started building a series of chapels at strategic points in his district.

His letters to the Fathers of the Sacred Hearts in Europe were sprinkled with requests. He needed catechisms, rosaries, building materials. And bells!

At home in Flanders, no village church, no matter how small, was without a bell. So each chapel at Puna, rough and crude though it might be, must have one too. The sound of bells, serving the practical purpose of calling the people to religious services, had also for Father Damien a deeper meaning. Each stroke was the signature of Christianity written upon a pagan land.

"Our poor islanders are very happy when they see Kamiano coming", Damien wrote. "And I, for my part, love them very much. I would gladly give my life for them, as our Savior did."

He tried to make the rounds of his big parish, preaching, teaching, baptizing, hearing confessions, and giving the Last Sacraments.

One day, as he returned on his horse from a sick call fifteen miles away, he found Father Clement waiting for him. He, too, was a father of the Sacred Hearts, stationed in the nearby district of Kohala. A visit from another priest was a rare occasion. Damien greeted Father Clement warmly.

"And how are things going at Kohala Mission?" he asked Father Clement.

The other priest shook his head wearily.

"Not well at all, Father Damien." Father Clement's face was white and drawn.

"What's the trouble?"

"It's too much for me. My health can't stand up under those long, hot trips. I don't want to give up the mission . . ."

Father Clement's territory took in the districts of Hamakua and Kohala—altogether about one-third of the island of Hawaii. It was much larger than Puna.

"Why not ask Bishop Maigret to let us change places?" Damien suggested. "I'm strong, thank God. So far, my health has been perfect. Let me take over Kohala, and you come here."

"That is very generous of you, Father Damien. It's true that here the work would not be so heavy. Perhaps I would get stronger."

Bishop Maigret agreed quickly to the change, and Damien, saying good-bye to the people of Puna, whom he had already grown to love, set out with his few possessions for his new parish of two thousand square miles!

Here he found only one church standing. Again he had to turn carpenter and contractor to build some chapels. Meanwhile, he celebrated Mass wherever he could—sometimes in the open air, sometimes in grass huts, or, if he found a crude schoolhouse, that would do very well.

In his new territory, Father Damien continued to travel from village to village to say Mass and to fill the spiritual needs of his people.

Early one morning, he stepped outside the grass hut in which he had slept and blew upon the curved shell that served as his church bell. It did not make a musical sound, as did the church bells of Belgium, but at least the people of the little village knew there would be Mass that day.

Petero had come out of the grass hut, too.

"I'll help you, if I may, Kamiano." He was a Hawaiian boy of about fourteen, the son of the man with whom Damien had stayed after the long horseback ride from the mission.

"Thank you, Petero." Damien was glad the boy had offered. Together they set up the portable altar under a large tree. Petero's mother brought armfuls of bright red flowers to decorate it. Soon the people began to arrive from the farthest end of the little settlement. Silently they gathered, kneeling around the altar, under the spreading branches of the tree.

Damien went into the hut to put on his vestments.

It was early morning, and the sun had just started to climb in the bright sky as the Mass began.

"I will go unto the altar of God . . ."

Petero served as altar boy. He had learned the responses well since Damien had begun visiting his village.

After Mass, everyone stayed for catechism. Damien went over the questions with them, and they recited the answers. Petero knew more of the answers than any of the others. Damien was pleased with the boy. After the lesson, he called Petero to him.

"You have certainly learned well the truths of your faith, Petero", Damien told him. "How would you like to be one of my missionary helpers?"

Petero's eyes lit up, and his handsome face was all smiles.

"Oh, if only I could, Kamiano!"

Damien explained his plan. Since it took the priest eight days to travel the entire length and breadth of the mission district, he could not always say Mass every Sunday in each village. So that the Christians of the various settlements would not forget about their faith in between his visits, Damien had taught some of the young men to be prayer leaders. They would blow the shell on Sunday morning, just as he did, calling the people to prayer. The catechist in each settlement would lead the prayers, go over the catechism, and perhaps give a short talk on some point of doctrine.

Petero was overjoyed to be chosen. Ever since the Kamiano had been coming to his village, he had wished the priest did not have to rush away so soon to the next station.

"But . . . but do you think I am good enough, Kamiano? I mean, there are many things I do not know about our holy religion."

"I'll teach you, Petero. Come back with me to the mission and stay a while. Let's go now, and ask your father's permission."

Petero's parents were putting the final touches to the big feast they had prepared in honor of Kamiano's visit. The food was spread out on the ground under the trees—roast pig, *poi* (a paste made from the taro root), many other delicious foods. The Hawaiian people loved their luau, as they called the feast, as much as the Belgians loved their *kermesse*.

Later in the day, Damien visited many of the grass huts of the village, hearing confessions, baptizing the new babies, and giving the last rites to the sick. Before he left, the altar was prepared once more, with Petero's help, and the people gathered for Benediction and the Rosary.

Then Damien said good-bye and packed up his Mass kit. Petero's father was glad to have his son go along too. Now the boy ran to get Damien's horse, tied securely to a tree behind the hut.

Damien strapped his Mass kit and other things firmly to the horse's saddle. He could not risk losing them on the rough trip ahead. Petero, too, had his horse ready, and together they set out across the mountainous land. The journey would take at least twenty-four hours; they would sleep somewhere under the open sky.

Damien was tired. Days of hard riding under the torrid sun and nights of sleeping on rocky earth had toughened his already strong body. But he was cheerful. Little by little, with more boys like Petero to help him, he would one day manage to minister to all his people.

He would build churches and chapels for them, as sturdy and beautiful as his work-roughened hands could make them. He would write once again to Belgium and beg them to send him bells.

A bell in every church tower, just as in Belgium! Soon, soon, he would have them ringing all over Hawaii!

7

PETERO'S PROBLEM

T<small>HAT'S ALL</small> for today, Petero", Damien said, shutting the Book of Gospels and rising from his chair. "You know, you're a very good pupil." The priest's eyes sparkled behind his thick, gold-rimmed glasses. "Pretty soon you'll be explaining this book better than I can."

Petero smiled, but he did not feel very happy.

"I'm going out to do some hoeing in the potato field now, Petero." Damien took off his glasses and put on his broad-brimmed hat. "Come along if you want to."

But Petero did not move as Damien went out of the room.

He was wondering whether it had been a good idea after all to come to stay in the priest's house at Vaiapuka and learn to be a prayer leader.

In Damien's five-room mission of pala leaves, Petero did not feel at home. Things seemed different, strange. He was lonely for his father and mother and his friends back in his own village.

Like most Hawaiians, Petero was generally cheerful and fun-loving. In the games and sports of the village, he was often the leader. He wondered now if being a prayer leader meant an end to all those good times. Soon it would be his job to blow the conch shell calling everyone to church. How would his friends feel when they saw him, Petero, standing up before everyone to lead the hymns?

"I could run away", he said to himself. He stood up and looked toward the open door. Over that way, past many hills, lay his home in Hamakua. But, no, he could not do that.

"Kamiano has been good to me", he thought. "He would be sad if I went away without telling him."

Petero walked slowly outside. Beneath his happy-go-lucky nature lay something much more serious. He was a true and sincere Christian. In the government school, he had learned some reading and writing from a Catholic teacher. He had a quick mind, as Kamiano had said. He did not listen any longer to the *kahunas*, the pagan priests who still practiced the native religion, which included human and animal sacrifices, idol worship, and belief in numerous gods and goddesses.

He paused a moment before Damien's mission church. It was the only church Petero had ever seen. He loved to serve High Mass on Sundays, when there was singing and the altar was bright with sweet-smelling flowers and lighted candles.

He wandered slowly along, scuffing his bare feet lazily through the dirt. *Makai*—toward the water. There, perhaps, he could think more clearly.

It was much later in the day when Damien set out to look for him. Petero had been missing all afternoon. Damien was thinking hard, as he strode rapidly along toward the shore.

"Maybe I hurry him too much. I am too anxious to teach him everything so he can go home and begin his work." Damien knew well this old failing of his—impatience. He smiled wryly to himself as he thought of his brother, Father Pamphile, now a theology professor back in Louvain. Here Damien had his class too—one pupil! He must write to Pamphile about it.

Had Petero run off home? Perhaps. It would be just one more disappointment for a missionary to put down to experience.

Just then he came to a clearing leading to the shore.

Down by the water, Petero sat forlornly on a steep rock. He was watching some fishermen haul in their net with the day's catch.

Damien stood beside Petero, watching the men deftly handle the weighted net.

"You, too, can be a fisherman", said the priest, quietly. "But you will catch fish much bigger than these!" He smiled at the boy huddled on the rock. Petero looked up suddenly, his dark eyes frankly questioning those of Damien.

"Do you—do you really believe I can do it?"

"I know you can, Petero", Damien told him.

They talked a long time, while the sun went down across the water, turning the whole world around them into red and gold.

"I loved good times and games, too, when I was your age, Petero. I still do. But I also wanted to become a priest. There were many things standing in my way, but, you see, I am here! That's because I was sure in my heart it was what God wanted me to do. Don't you feel sure that God wants you to be his helper among your people?"

"I do believe it—now", said Petero with certainty. The bell rang in the mission church. It was time for evening services. Petero did not feel lonely anymore. The Kamiano did not seem like a foreign stranger to him but a friend who knew what was in his heart.

He did not feel like running away again. There were many new and interesting things to do at Vaiapuka.

Damien and he shared the same simple meals of meat, bread, *poi*, and more *poi*. Sometimes there was hot, rich coffee. Petero helped Damien look after his fields of beans, sweet potatoes, and tobacco. He liked to feed the horses and mules, the chickens and sheep.

"How do you like my farm?" Damien would ask.

Petero, who had never seen such a farm before, would only answer with a smile, as he watched Damien making altar candles from beeswax or gathering honey from his hives.

Soon the day came for Petero to return to his village.

"Before you go, there is a favor I want to ask", Damien said. "Promise me that you and the other Christians of your village will build a chapel. Let it be an act of thanksgiving for having received the Catholic faith."

"I promise, Father Damien", Petero answered. "When you come to see us next time, we shall have the wood ready for the building—only first we must have some land."

"Leave that to me, Petero. I intend to write a letter to the queen asking for a grant of land in your village."

"Your blessing, please, Kamiano, before I go." Petero knelt on the ground and bowed his head as Damien blessed him. Then he was on his horse and away.

Damien turned his steps back to his house. He would write some letters today; he was arranging to trade some of his tobacco to a merchant in Hilo in return for some paint for his new chapels. This was one way he could obtain supplies without going into debt, for the Fathers of the Sacred Hearts had many missions to support and could not always meet Damien's requests for building materials.

In Honolulu, through the sisters of the Sacred Hearts, who had their convent in the capital, he had traded part of his sweet-potato crop for biscuits, wheat, and rice. In this way he managed to support himself. In terms of money, he was very poor, but he grew most of his food, and his own needs were very few, for he had adopted simple Hawaiian ways of living.

The next day was Saturday, and Father Damien was up early to go to a very distant and isolated part of his immense "parish". It was a little Christian settlement bordered by rough seas, almost inaccessible by land. No road led there.

Down by the shore two young men worked over their canoe of *koa*, Hawaiian mahogany. It was really nothing more than a hollowed-out tree about five feet wide. Explaining where he wanted to go, Damien asked if they would take him.

"To go over the mountains would be a trip of several days," he told them, "but if I go by the sea route I can be there in time for Sunday Mass."

They agreed to take him.

Damien strapped his luggage firmly inside the canoe. His heart was light as he got ready to leave, but he remembered to make his usual act of contrition just before climbing into the small vessel and settling himself for the voyage.

In a few minutes, they were headed straight out to sea. The muscles stood out sharply on the brown arms of the crewmen as they rowed rapidly along. The canoe slid smoothly through the calm, blue water. In the distance, they could see the mountains, misty and far away. It was a perfect day to set out. Damien thought of the lonely little settlement toward which he was heading. It was seldom that a priest was able to get to see these people. Yet everyone—or nearly everyone—in the settlement had been baptized!

Suddenly, the canoe turned sharply, veering away from its steady course. The two Hawaiians struggled with all their strength to bring their vessel around, but they could not. A whirling current caught it. In a moment, the canoe had turned over, flinging everyone into the sea.

The two islanders shouted wildly as they floundered about in the water trying to right their capsized canoe. Damien tried to help, but none of them knew how get it upright again without filling it with water. Damien was thankful that at least he had learned to swim back home on the Dyle River.

"Head the canoe back toward shore", he shouted to the others. "We can pull it with one hand and swim with the other." He showed them what he meant. They followed his example. It was awkward, but, after what seemed like a very long time, they finally succeeded in reaching shore.

After they had pulled the canoe up on the beach,

Damien wearily unstrapped his luggage. Fortunately, he had tied it firmly; nothing had been lost. Only his small breviary, which he carried everywhere with him, was soaked with sea water. He could never use it again!

Off he went toward home, still dripping from head to foot. That was enough traveling for one day! But the thought of the village he had wanted to visit could not be put out of his mind. He felt certain that he should go there right away. A few days later, he set out again, by land this time, riding one of his horses, with his knapsack strapped to his back.

It took him four days, clinging to the spiny backs of huge rocks, twisting up and down the sides of deep cliffs and valleys. For a time he rode stubbornly over the rough land, staking out his horse to graze at night. When he was tired and hungry, he knew he could find a warm welcome at any hut along his way. If there was none, he slept on the ground under the bare sky.

Then he had to leave his horse to be looked after by some villagers and go ahead on foot. At one place he crossed, by wading and swimming, a long, inward-stretching finger of the sea. In the darkness of the uplands, he waded through miles of mud. The rain sloshed down around him, heavier, wetter, than any Belgian rain. At last he found the village, a small group of huts huddled together at the foot of a steep mountain. One more sharp downward path, and he came to a thatched house. A little child played before the hut in the mud. She looked up, startled to see a white man, and darted quickly away to tell her mother. Word spread through the village that the priest had come at last! Everyone ran out to greet him. A young woman with a baby in her arms pushed her way through her gathering neighbors to Damien.

She was crying.

"Kamiano—look! My baby is very sick. Please baptize him right away."

Damien saw at a glance that the baby had not much longer to live. It took him only a few moments to baptize him, right there in the muddy road.

As soon as the priest had finished, the baby gave a little gasp and lay very still in his mother's arms. Damien suddenly knew why he had felt so strongly that he must come to this village. He was thankful he had arrived in time.

As the saddened mother turned away, other villagers noticed that the priest's feet were bare and bleeding. His boots had long since been torn to bits on jagged rocks, and his hands, by which he had clung to the craggy mountainsides, were bruised and cut. They led him away to rest. They brought him fish and *poi* and tried to make him comfortable.

But he had not come there to rest. Soon he was up again, eager to see them all. First, he went to visit all the sick. He preached, he baptized, he taught catechism, heard confessions, and celebrated Holy Mass each morning at his outdoor altar.

The simple hospitality of the people and their child-like joy in having him with them for a while was all the reward Damien wanted on these hard journeys around his mission territory. He only wished he might be everywhere at once, doing everything that he saw should be done.

Here the prayer leaders were a great help. He had several, but Petero was, by far, the best. He had become a fine speaker, and all the people of the village, both Christian and non-Christian, went to hear him. Some were convinced that he spoke the truth. To those who wished to become Christians, he gave regular instructions. Damien, when he came, usually found them waiting to be baptized.

In Petero's village, Damien celebrated Mass in an abandoned schoolhouse, a straw hut with a door only about four feet high. He had to stoop low to get his big frame inside. Then, all during Mass, the wind kept blowing through the doorway, and the candles went out again and again.

"What about the chapel you promised me, Petero?" he asked afterward.

"We have the wood all ready, Kamiano," Petero answered, "but we have no land. Besides, we don't know how to build a church."

Damien took a letter from his black cassock. "I have a grant of six hundred acres from the queen", he said. "All we need is a plan for the building."

Petero and some of the other young men of the village watched as Damien, on the back of his letter, drew rough plans for a simple frame church. It would have a gable on the front and, on the top, a large wooden cross.

The next day they began work. Damien showed his helpers how to lay the foundation and mount the framework. He himself nailed on the roof. Petero worked on the cross, more than six feet tall, that would crown their church. One day, when the building was nearly done, Petero brought one of his friends to Damien.

"This is Ahumaino", Petero explained. "He's a very good painter. He can carve in wood, too. He wants to make decorations for our church."

Ahumaino, small and quick, was a gifted artist. He loved bright colors. The little church took on a festive look under his brush. Ahumaino laughed often, and his dark eyes would dance as he teased Damien about a surprise he was planning for the priest.

"Wait and see, Kamiano", Ahumaino would say. Damien would try to guess what it was. Some of his guesses were so funny that everyone listening would laugh. When Damien laughed, he could be heard all over the village!

Then one day Ahumaino brought his "surprise". Shyly, he showed it to Damien. It was a figure of the Blessed Mother, carved of *koa*. She had the large eyes and soft features of a lovely Hawaiian woman.

"Here, Kamiano. I made it for the church. Is it good enough?" Damien was delighted. He would be sure to give it a place of honor.

Soon it was time for the blessing of the finished building. Bishop Maigret came. As usual, he was in a hurry to get on to the next mission. He wanted to hold the consecration right away, but the people of the village would not hear of it. This would not be the proper way to celebrate such an important event, they thought. They begged him to stay for ten days so that they could prepare a proper feast. Neighbors for miles around were invited to attend, and a whole herd of pigs was killed to be roasted for the luau.

Petero was exultant. The completion of the beautiful new church seemed to crown all his efforts as a prayer leader. Never, he thought, had there been such a feast in his village before. Petero had never felt happier. Now the Christians had something right in their midst that would always remind them of their faith. They looked up to Petero as their leader.

"You have done your work well, Petero", Damien told him. "Remember, I told you you could do it", he said with a smile.

Petero smiled back. "I'm glad. I'm glad I didn't run away from Vaiapuka that day."

8

SHADOWS OF THE GRAY ISLAND

A T Kohala, time moved by almost unnoticed. Years
passed. Damien, still in his twenties, could call
himself a seasoned missionary. To those who knew him,
he was many men.

To his islanders, he was a friend and spiritual father,
generous, self-sacrificing, understanding, full of lively
good humor.

To his superiors in the religious Congregation of the Sacred Hearts, he was a zealous and enthusiastic missionary. True, he seemed at times a bit too impatient to get things done. He needed to be slowed down here and there. Yet his record showed many converts. Under his direction, the faith had spread. And always he kept the spirit of obedience to those whom God had placed over him.

To his family back in Belgium, he was still the impetuous Joseph, the strong and handsome son, the adventurous brother who had bravely followed a divine call to the distant islands of the Pacific.

To himself he was a hard-riding, hard-praying, hard-hammering man, with a good share of faults and failures. But he was unwavering in his priestly dedication, willing to give his life, if necessary, to its fulfillment.

Sometimes he was lonely, tired, discouraged. Much as he loved the Hawaiians and their colorful country, he never forgot the flat plains and quiet rivers of his native land.

His letters home were full of chatty details, often touched with homesickness.

"I got your letter at one of the ports", he wrote to Father Pamphile. "All night, as I crossed the lava of a new volcano, I thought over the news you had sent. Now I was at the mill in Betecom with Leonce and Gerard, now at the bedside of Henri Winokx . . . now with Pauline in her convent. . . . Where are those happy times, my dear brother, living under our parents' care. . . .

The beautiful time of our childhood and youth have passed! It is now the time of manhood, when we have to work courageously in the vineyard of the Lord."

One evening, after darkness had fallen, Damien rode into Petero's village. As usual, he went to the hut of Petero's father and mother first. As he bent to enter, he saw that they greeted him sadly, without their customary welcoming smiles. Petero was nowhere to be seen.

"Where is Petero?" Damien asked. "I want to talk with him about preparing the confirmation class. Bishop Maigret will soon be passing through this part of the country."

A strange look came over the faces of Petero's parents—a look of terror. Finally, the father spoke, leaning across to Damien and whispering, as if afraid he might be overheard.

"He's gone. The police are looking for him."

"Police? But what . . ."

"*Maipake!*" The mother began to cry quietly.

Damien looked up in shock and amazement. *Maipake* was a word spoken with dread and horror by every Hawaiian. It meant the most terrible doom they knew. "Separating sickness" they called it, for it was not so much the lingering death, the ugly disfigurement it could bring, or even the fact that it could not be cured that alarmed the people so much. It was because to be a victim of *maipake* meant to be perpetually exiled. It meant never to see one's family and friends again. In 1865, alarm over the rapid spread of the disease throughout the islands had caused the Hawaiian government to pass a law that all those who contracted it must spend the rest of their lives in a special colony on the island of Molokai.

Damien knew very well what that meant. Riding from village to village on his apostolic rounds, he had heard many terrible stories that drifted back from Molokai. It was now becoming known instead as "The Gray Island", for the Hawaiian government, anxious only to protect the healthy population by isolating the sick, had given little thought to the welfare of the exiles. Poverty, hunger, lack of any doctor or medical care were added to the quite sufficient suffering of an incurable disease. No wonder those who went there—and some of them had been Damien's own parishioners—quickly forgot Christian ways of living.

And now *maipake*—the age-old scourge of leprosy—had taken Petero! Damien rode sorrowfully back to Vaiapuka. Full of his own reflections, he did not notice the strange stillness hanging in the air.

Suddenly the earth beneath him seemed to tremble. It was only for a moment. He was riding into his own gate then, and he felt the weight of the motionless atmosphere pressing down upon his tired body.

He did not know it, but a hundred miles away, moving along its deadly path across the Pacific, a typhoon advanced toward Hawaii!

That day the earth quaked again and again with growing violence. The people became frightened.

"The gods are angry!" they cried. "We must appease them."

Hastily the *kahunas* led the pagan rites and sacrifices. But even as they danced and chanted, louder than the *uli-uli* drums sounded the muffled roar Hawaiians knew so well and feared so much. Like sleeping giants roused to anger, the ancient volcanoes were awakening. Smoke began to pour from the craters, and the boiling lava made the mountainsides red. Weird fires, orange, purple, and crimson, burned high on the peaks.

"Pele! Pele! Spare us", the people cried to the goddess of the volcano. They ran about in panic. Some tried to take refuge in caves.

The island rocked like a canoe in stormy seas. It was shaken from coast to coast by the earthquake. After that came the rivers of lava, five miles wide in some places, swallowing up villages, herds, and people. And then the typhoon struck with dizzying weight.

All the forces of nature were combined to destroy them, it seemed. Damien waited in the darkness of Vaiapuka. The wind tore at every wall, flattening the fragile grass huts by the hundreds. He thought of his churches, built with so much love and labor. In his own little steeple he heard, above the high-singing wind, his chapel bells clanging wildly without any human touch. He thought of his people, seeking shelter where there was none. Hawaiian villages were never built to stand up against such storms.

As soon as the wind began to subside, Damien started

out to bring help to the survivors. Loaded down with food and clothing, he went into the outlying country. His horse picked its way through gray seas of just-cooled lava, under whose fiery tides many lay dead. In one place, he saw the side of a mountain sheared off, as if by a giant knife. He hurried to give the last rites to the dying. Many settlements had completely disappeared in the path of the whirlwind. Whole forests had been uprooted, leaving Damien to find his way among the great trees, lying on their sides.

After the emergency, Damien had to make plans for the rebuilding of the churches, schools, and other buildings that had gone down in ruins. He was not discouraged, for, after all, he had been spared. More and more he missed his best helper, Petero.

In one place a man said to him, "Kamiano, you come to us on your horse, and then you ride away again. People ask, 'Where does the Kamiano really live?'" Damien smiled and pointed to his saddle. "That's my home", he said, and then added, "Of course, I have my house at the mission, but I spend most of my time right here." At times he would be traveling for six weeks at a time. Like all the Hawaiian missionaries, he made it a habit not to carry provisions.

He never minded going out at any time, day or night, to help someone in need. One night, his mount suddenly ran wild and carried Damien ten miles from home. Tired out at last, the animal came to a halt on a mountaintop. Darkness had fallen. Damien did not know just where he was, and he was wet and hungry. Just then, a dog barked in the distance. What a welcome sound!

"Where there's a dog, there must be people", Damien said to himself.

He started in the direction of the bark. It came again, right in front of him. After groping and stumbling in the pitch blackness for a time, he came to a small hut.

The dog barked loudly as the priest came up to the door. A man put his head out. Damien tried to make himself heard above the dog's barking. The man could not hear him very well, but, with true Hawaiian hospitality, he invited him to come in.

"Kamiano?" the man said finally. He could see that his visitor was a priest, although he himself was not a Christian. "Stay here tonight. In the morning you can find your way home." The man lived alone there with his dog and his little herd of sheep. "You are welcome, Kamiano."

Damien was glad, not only to have a place to stay for the night, but to have a chance to speak with his host. His missionary spirit never allowed him to waste any opportunity to speak about the faith, in season or out of season. Generally, people listened gladly, for he had a lively and persuasive way of speaking.

Often it took all of Damien's Flemish good sense to solve the problems of church-building in a land that seemed to be all up-and-down. The Hawaiians were not fond of hard physical work as a rule, but, with Damien tackling the toughest jobs himself, they were encour-

aged to do their best. One afternoon, the priest and his
band of helpers stood looking at the foundation of a new
church they had just laid far up on a mountain. At the
foot of the mountains, the sea lay blue and clear.

"How can we build a church here, Kamiano?" one of
the men asked. "The wood is all down on the beach,
where it was unloaded from the boat."

"Yes," put in another, "and the way up here is so steep
that my three pairs of oxen can hardly pull up an empty
cart."

They looked at one another, puzzled, but Damien,
after thinking a few minutes, had an answer.

"Tonight, before sundown, we can all go down to the
beach and sleep in the open. Then, after morning
prayers, each one will take a piece of lumber and start up
here. When the work is finished for the day, we can have
evening services before starting down again. Next day
we can do it all over again."

The lumber lay neatly piled, cut to proper length, on
the beach. Damien always picked the largest pieces for
his trip up the rocky mountainside in the broiling sun.

Bishop Maigret had once spoken of the young priest's
amazing strength.

"The natives are everlastingly astonished at him! They
shout as though it is a miracle when they watch him
carry a huge beam that three or four of them could
hardly lift!"

But if the vicar apostolic of the Hawaiian Islands
admired Damien's energy, there were others who found

it hard to keep up with the pace he set for himself. One of these was Father Modeste, in Honolulu, who was in charge of the Hawaiian missions of the Sacred Hearts Fathers. He found it very hard to say no to Damien's constant begging for help in his church building. After all, there were many missions to be maintained from Father Modeste's modest funds. But Damien always, or nearly always, won out in his pleas. When he wanted permission to begin a chapel at Kahuahale, he wrote movingly: "Kahuahale is a little hill next to a spring that has water even in the dry season. Christians live all around it. You can see the chapel from the sea. The ship going from Maui to Kona will see it. From Kona to Vaimea it is continually in view as you go through the terrible reefs of Kiholo. . . ."

Then, one day, he came home to find a letter waiting for him. It brought cheerful news. The church that the Sacred Hearts Fathers had been building for the past six years at Wailuku was finished at last! Bishop Maigret would be there for the consecration. It was to be a triumphant celebration. Damien, together with other priests of the islands, was invited to attend the ceremonies. Wailuku was some distance away from Kohala, on the island of Maui.

On a sunny day in May 1873, Damien boarded the ramshackle island steamer for the trip to Wailuku. As the shores of Kohala disappeared behind him, a strange feeling of sadness came upon Damien. Some inner voice was telling him, "This is good-bye to Kohala forever!"

Tears came to his eyes even at the thought of leaving the people who had become so dear to him. He loved them deeply. He loved the little chapels he had built for them. He could never forget Petero and the others who had been sent into exile. Across the water there, on the "Gray Island" of Molokai, they were living out miserable lives of loneliness and pain.

But he must shake his head roughly and drive off such gloomy thoughts. There was no time for them today, he reminded himself sharply. He would be away only a few days. The blessing of the new church marked a happy milestone for the work of the Congregation of the Sacred Hearts in the islands.

Damien glanced once more in the wake of the steamer. Kohala was no longer to be seen. Like a dream, it had vanished and, with it, nine years of Damien's priestly life. It was as if the blue Pacific had quietly closed over it, leaving the bells of his churches to ring eerily under the sea.

Soon the voices of the choir at Wailuku were ringing joyfully. The altar was splendid with rich altar cloths and brilliant tropical flowers. Bishop Maigret, in his flowing vestments, spoke the solemn words of the consecration in his clear voice: "Lord, send your Spirit from heaven to make this church an ever-holy place, and this altar a ready table for the sacrifice of Christ."

Damien knelt in the sanctuary. Scenes of his own missionary life passed through his mind, as he joined his prayers with those of his fellow priests. The choir sang the Offertory: "O Lord God, in the simplicity of my heart I have joyously offered all things to you. . . ."

Yes, everything, he thought with gratitude—the long tiring journeys, painful hardships, profound joys.

After Mass, there was a happy reunion. The four younger priests had much to talk over—Father Gulstan, a Frenchman who spoke Hawaiian very well and was much loved in the islands; Father Boniface and Father Rupert, who had come from Germany, and Father Damien,

They talked a while of this and that, telling of their experiences. They even joked a bit about Bishop Maigret's aged mule.

"How is Kapakahi?" The mule was famous throughout the archipelago.

"Getting old, like his master." Bishop Maigret himself had come into the room. "But, like me, he keeps going."

The missionary bishop, though well along in years, was still one of the best riders of the mission band. *Lui ka Epikopo*—"Louis, the bishop"—the Hawaiians called him.

Bishop Maigret suddenly turned to the younger men, his face very serious.

"There is something I must speak to you about today," the old bishop began, "something I do not want to say, but I am afraid I must."

They waited silently.

"I've thought it over for some time. I've prayed. I can't avoid the issue any longer. The Molokai colonists need a priest. They need a priest more than all the other people of the Hawaiian Islands put together!

"More and more poor people are being sent there every day. Because of their illness and the bad living conditions in the colony, they die very fast. We cannot leave them abandoned any longer."

Bishop Maigret went on to explain that he had received many urgent messages from the exiles, begging for a priest. "As you know, Brother Bertrand went there to build a chapel. They asked him to speak to me on his return. They told him, 'Talk to Lui ka Epikopo. Tell him it isn't enough for us to see a priest once a year. We have too much time to die between visits. How can we save our souls without a priest?'

"I can no longer avoid answering that question", he concluded. "Yet—I haven't the cruelty to command any one of you to make this sacrifice."

It was not the first time the question had come up. Each of the young priests was ready to go. They said so now again.

A strange expression, determined, lit by some inner fire, burned on Damien's face. He spoke up quickly.

"Let me go to Molokai, Your Lordship."

"You know what this means, Father Damien. Once there, you'll have little contact with the mainland. You will not be able to go back and forth freely."

"I know that, Your Lordship. I also know some of the people there. They were once my own parishioners." He was thinking especially of Petero.

"You must realize, Father Damien, that you will be putting yourself in grave danger of contracting an incurable disease."

"On the day of my religious profession, Your Lordship, I remember I was covered by a funeral pall. So I willingly accept this second death . . ."

"Very well, then." Bishop Maigret had once more his usual briskness. He was much relieved to have settled the problem that had worried him so much. At least, it was settled for the time being. He was pleased and edified by the bravery of his young missionaries, but, quite evidently, he realized, Father Damien believed himself mysteriously called to the heroic undertaking.

"The steamer *Kilauea* leaves soon for Molokai. I'll go with you. Can you be ready in a few hours?"

"I'm ready now, Your Lordship", answered Damien.

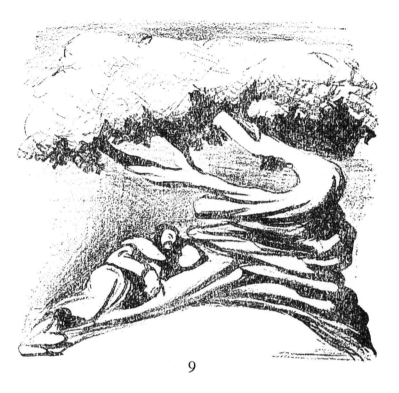

9

NIGHT UNDER THE
PANDANUS TREE

THE RAIN had stopped toward morning. Kaimu awoke and looked across the wet beach out to sea. Far off, coming slowly toward him, was the ship *Kilauea*. Kaimu raised himself on his elbow and watched it. The coarse grass mat under him was still wet from the night's downpour. Above him, thousands of feet up the cliffs, or *palis*, the clouds still hung low over Molokai. Kaimu lay back on his damp resting place and stared at the *palis*, their tops now hidden in gray mists, like veils.

He wondered again what lay on the other side of that wall of stone that cut off the rest of the island of Molokai as though it did not even exist. Were there villages there? He had heard that there were. Boys over there probably had mothers and fathers and their own places in the corner of the grass hut.

Kaimu's memories of his own home were very dim. It must have been years since the police had come, taken him out of his mother's arms, and roughly put him on the boat. There had been crying and moaning, then a long journey over dark water. Then . . .

Kaimu shook off his dreams and jumped to his feet. If the *Kilauea* were coming, he'd better let the old man know. His arms and legs ached from lying on the rain-soaked beach. He ran toward the little cluster of tumble-down shacks that made up the village of the sick—Kalaupapa. The old man lay moaning restlessly in his hut. The roof was partly caved in, and water dripped slowly on the littered floor.

The old man could not walk anymore. "You, Kaimu, are my legs now", he would tell the boy, and a strange glitter would come into his feverish eyes.

He had taught Kaimu many things—how to steal food boxes from the boats and how to hold the half-full gourd to his lips and drink the burning *ki* liquor that made Kaimu's head spin and his hands and feet forget to obey him.

Now the old man squinted up at Kaimu in the dim and bad-smelling air of the hut.

"The boat's coming in. I saw it far out, just turning in", Kaimu said breathlessly.

"Mind you work fast then, boy. If there's food on board, watch till you see them start to unload. Slip up behind them and take whatever you can. Bring it here as fast as you can run. See that they don't catch you, either."

Kaimu had to lean close to the old man to hear what he was saying, for the sickness had taken away his voice. He could only whisper now, and, in a way, it was better, for he could not shout at Kaimu anymore.

"All right. I'll go." Kaimu ran out again into the gray morning. As he went he shouted, "Boat's coming! Boat's coming!"

Soon everyone who could walk was down at the beach to see the *Kilauea* in. It was the only bit of excitement in their dreary lives. But for the occasional coming of the boat, the outer world—the world of hope, health, and love—might never have been there at all.

Kaimu darted here and there. The sickness did not bother him much yet. He had never seen his face, for Kalaupapa had no mirrors. He did not know whether it looked bad or not. He was only a little lame. Sometimes he stumbled and fell because of his weakened foot.

The whistle of the *Kilauea* was long, low, and sad. Its sound, as the vessel drew into Kalaupapa harbor, was mixed with the mooing of fifty cows on board, shipped to Molokai by the government to provide some milk.

Kaimu made a face. Who wanted milk? He couldn't remember when he had last had any. After all, he couldn't very well steal a cow.

Now came the second herd. These were the passengers, a load of newly captured sick people being unceremoniously introduced to their future home—six square miles of barren beach, overshadowed always by the *palis*.

"Look. There's Lui ka Epikopo!" shouted someone on shore.

"Somebody's with him." They watched with interest as the two men in clerical clothing walked down the gangplank. Visitors were almost unheard of at Kalaupapa. No wonder! It was a place everyone made certain to stay far away from. Besides, the government did not allow contact with the outside world.

A man hurried through the waiting crowd with a paper in his hand.

"Sign it! Sign it!" he was saying. "We're giving a petition to Louis, the bishop, asking him to send us a priest." Some had not the hands to hold the pen. Others helped them.

Kaimu watched closely to see if any food boxes would be taken off the ship. He was ready to make his haul quickly and get away to the old man's hut. But he stopped just a moment to watch the old bishop and the young priest who walked beside him to the shore.

The man with the petition broke through the others. He knelt on the wet sand at Bishop Maigret's feet.

"Here, Bishop Maigret, from the Christians of Molokai . . ."

The bishop glanced quickly at the paper and then held up his hand for silence. The lines of age on his forehead looked deeper than usual. He spoke slowly.

"My dear children," he began, just as he had begun so many sermons in his long missionary life. "I have brought you a priest. He will be a father to you all." He turned to Damien beside him. He meant to say more, to tell them his name, of his concern for their souls, but he found he could say no more.

The whistle of the *Kilauea* sounded again. It was ready to leave. No vessel ever stayed longer in Kalaupapa harbor than was absolutely necessary. The crew wanted to get off to more cheerful ports.

Bishop Maigret raised his hand once more, and his lips moved silently as he pronounced the words of blessing over the people and over Damien kneeling before him. He turned quickly and went toward the ship, not looking around again. Some of the people threw themselves in his path with tears of gratitude. Again and again he traced the Sign of the Cross wordlessly in the air. Then he mounted the gangplank and, with faltering steps, took his place on deck.

The *Kilauea* weighed anchor and turned away, back to the land of the living. On the miserable beach of Kalaupapa, Damien stood face-to-face with the living dead!

He saw before him faces and bodies scarred and made

ugly by disease. Because of the wonderful gift of divine grace, he saw more. He saw also the souls of God's abandoned, but beloved, children, pleading with him for their eternal salvation.

He had not come to save their bodies. Medical science had not yet learned how to do that. But their souls could never be destroyed by any illness save that of sin and despair. In heaven, each one could hope for a glorious welcome when the trial of his life on earth was done.

The people watched him with suspicion in their eyes. Thankful as they were to have a priest come to stay among them, one question now came to every mind. Would he, like all other healthy men, turn away from them in fear and disgust? They could hardly believe otherwise, for they had learned in bitterness that they were outcasts, hated and feared by the whole world.

Kaimu stood a little way off, watching with narrow, stealthy eyes. This newcomer brought no baggage, so there was nothing Kaimu could steal. The old man would be angry. The boat had brought no provisions. Kaimu was afraid to go back empty-handed.

Perhaps, Kaimu thought, the strange white man had something of value hidden somewhere about him— money in his pocket, or a gold watch. He never took his dark, watchful eyes from the priest as Damien turned and, with long quick strides, began to walk toward the settlement.

It was while he was walking that Damien came upon the little chapel of Saint Philomena that Brother Bertrand had built the year before. Like everything else he saw around him, it was run-down and neglected. Damien leaned over and cleared a handful of trash from the door. Inside, it was the same. He broke a branch from a nearby tree and, using it as a broom, began to sweep the floor of the tiny chapel.

Many people had followed him silently from the beach, and they now stood around in a circle, watching his every move. The hazy mist of early morning had cleared away, and the hot sun streamed down. Drops of sweat soon stood out on Damien's broad forehead.

They watched him doubtfully. They hung back from speaking to him. Some might have felt like running to him and asking his blessing. Some might have kissed his hands in gratitude just for coming to their lonely place of exile. Some would have begged him to go with them right away to the hut of one close to death. Others, who were not Christians, watched him with bitterness in their eyes. They cared for nothing but their own lawless ways. If this stranger intended to keep them from their usual pleasures, they would see to it that he gave them little trouble!

"He must be hungry", a woman said finally. She had recognized Damien, for she had come from Kohala too. She went away and returned in a few minutes with some fruit. She herself did not suffer from leprosy but had come to the colony to care for her husband, who was a victim. Still, she was afraid the priest would refuse to take the food. Kaimu stood near her.

"Here," she said to the boy, "take this to the Kamiano."

Kaimu's eyes lighted up. There was a hard glint in them. He did not care whether the priest took the food or not, but perhaps Kaimu would have a chance to look for the gold watch.

Damien stood up to wipe his brow with his big handkerchief. Kaimu stood before him holding out the fruit without a word.

Damien's red face broke into a friendly smile.

"For me?" He reached out without hesitation and took the fruit from Kaimu's hands. "Thank you, . . ." he paused, waiting for the name.

"Kaimu", said the boy. He watched the priest with sharp, searching eyes. The old man would be pleased if Kaimu could bring home a European watch. They sometimes had great value.

"Thanks, Kaimu", said Damien. "Will you share it with me?"

Damien sat down on the ground. Kaimu, too surprised to refuse, sat beside him. A gasp of amazement went through the tense watchers. So he was not afraid of them after all! Perhaps this Kamiano they had so often dreamed of had come to them as a true friend.

Kaimu was still suspicious.

"Is your mother here? Did she give you this food?" asked Damien kindly.

"No."

"Your father—he is here with you, then?" Damien asked again.

"No."

"Then, who looks after you?" asked the priest.

"Oh—sometimes the old man does", Kaimu answered carelessly. Then he hurried to add, "I can take care of myself."

"I see. And where do you live, Kaimu?"

The boy waved his arm vaguely toward the beach.

"Out there. I sleep in the open."

If Damien was surprised at the story, he did not show any such thing. He had finished his lunch now, and he stood up to go on with the work. Saint Philomena's would be ready for Mass in the morning.

"Do you want to help me?" Damien asked, as he took up his tree-branch broom again.

For a moment, Kaimu wondered, "What will the old man say?" But then the ugly face in the dark hut was blotted out in Kaimu's mind by the strong, handsome features of Damien, who smiled, yes, smiled, at him!

Kaimu jumped up.

"I'll look for some flowers", he said and ran off.

As the early shadows lengthened across the *palis*, shutting out the afternoon sun, Kaimu brought a few flowers he had been able to find on the lower levels of the cliff. Someone else brought a faded roll of red crepe paper to wind around the plain candlesticks. Brother Bertrand's rather crude chapel began to take on a new dignity.

Saint Philomena's was a poor sanctuary at best, but it would do until Damien could build a proper church.

Already his head was full of plans. Kaimu—there must be many like him—Kaimu must have a home, someone to look after him. Tomorrow he must begin visiting the huts of his people, one by one, along the ragged settlement. First, he must find the sickest, the most abandoned, the most forlorn.

For today he could do no more. He looked about for a place to spend the night. Near Saint Philomena's was an old pandanus tree, spreading its gnarled branches. On the big flat rock beneath it, Damien made his simple meal. Then he took out his breviary. That and his rosary were the only things he had brought with him to Molokai.

It was very dark now, and a kind of quiet had fallen, broken by weird sounds—the moans of the helpless sick, the boisterous laughter of those determined to forget their awful fate.

He lay on the bare ground, on the hard twisted roots of the pandanus, which gnarled themselves into a thick network above the soggy ground.

Tomorrow he must write for supplies. The list was forming swiftly in his tired mind—wine, hosts, religious books, rosaries, and, oh, yes, a clean shirt and a razor—and a bell for the new Saint Philomena's that he would build!

Kaimu did not go back to the old man's hut that night. As he stretched out on the beach, he felt almost happy. Impatiently, he waited for morning, when he and the Kamiano would work together again. Kaimu's eyelids were heavy with sleep, and beneath them his eyes had lost that steely shine.

Damien heard close by the lonely sound of surf, booming on the barren shore. Belgium had never seemed so far away.

10

THE ROSARY AND THE HAMMER

ANYBODY here?"

The hut was simply a lean-to of branches, rudely thatched with cane leaves. Damien had to bend over and hunch his big shoulders to get inside. In the darkness, he saw nothing at first—only a bundle of rags in the corner. As he looked more carefully, the bundle of rags seemed to be moving. He stepped closer.

It was not the first time he had seen such a strange sight. His first work after arriving at Molokai had been to visit the sick wherever they lay. Only his holy mission—the search for souls—enabled him to face the sights, sounds, and smells of those miserable hovels.

Kaimu had told Damien about this one, the last of the ragged line along the path that connected the two settlements, Kalawao and Kalaupapa. Damien knew already about the young man who spoke to no one and whose name nobody knew. He never left his hut, though Kaimu said he could walk very well. A woman left food outside for him nearly every day. Sometimes he took it, sometimes not.

Now he lay with his face turned away so that Damien could see nothing but the ragged cover. Perhaps he was asleep.

Damien spoke quietly.

"It's the priest, my son."

There was no movement. Then the voice came—dull, lifeless.

"No priest comes here."

"Yes, my son. I came here. Can I help you?"

Suddenly the form on the ground turned. The young man raised his head and stared at the priest as if he were a ghost.

"Kamiano?" His voice was unbelieving.

"That's right." Damien leaned closer. "Petero!"

The young man fell back on his pallet.

"I *was* Petero. Why did you come here, anyway?"

Damien had heard before that note of hopelessness, that utter despair. He had heard it in almost every one of the huts he had visited. Like a continual refrain, it seemed to echo the length and breadth of the desolate peninsula: "What's the use? What's the use?"

"Perhaps I came to find you, Petero", Damien answered. "I missed you at Kohala, you know. What happened? How did you come here?"

Petero told Damien the story—how he had run away from home when he had discovered the signs of *maipake* on his face. Deep in a wild ravine, he had hidden in a cave. At night his father or older brother would slip out and bring him food. This went on for many days, but the police did not give up their search. One night, suspecting his hiding place, they had followed Peter's father out of the village. There they had finally seized him and put him aboard the ship for Molokai.

Damien had heard such stories many times already. Sometimes the police had used bloodhounds in tracking down the sick. They were treated like criminals being banished to prison rather than like persons in need of special love and care.

"And now," Petero ended his sad story, "here I am, useless to myself, to everyone." He lay back and closed his eyes again.

As for Damien, finding Petero again was a wonderful surprise! He had often wondered what had become of his young friend and helper. He had not even known whether Petero was still alive or whether he had ever reached the gray shores of Molokai. Damien had never needed Petero's help so badly.

There were about two hundred Christians in the colony, and many more were now asking for instructions. Damien was kept busy from morning till night visiting the sick and caring for them spiritually and materially. He had no time to organize the catechism classes that were so much needed. Then, too, there were the children—boys and girls who, like Kaimu, had no fathers or mothers to care for them. They needed a teacher.

"Don't say you are useless, Petero. Finding you here is the best thing that has happened to me so far", Damien told his friend cheerfully. It was hard to find anything cheerful or amusing in his present circumstances, but Damien knew that he must not forget to laugh. He had come to bring hope to people whose laughter had been silenced too long.

"What can I do for you or anyone, now?" Petero answered sadly.

"Why, come on, and I'll show you."

"I—I can't come with you." Petero showed little interest in Damien's plans.

"Can't you walk?" Damien wanted to know.

"I don't know. I never try." Damien saw that Petero was not really very ill. His disease had so far had little effect on his body, but, as so often happened, it had been far more destructive to his mind. Like so many others, Petero believed his life had ended the moment he stepped ashore at Molokai.

Damien had to return again and again to talk to Petero and urge him to take up his work as a prayer leader. Gradually, the priest was able to renew Petero's interest in teaching, and Kaimu was his first pupil. In the beginning, the lessons were held outside Petero's hut, but, as other boys joined the group, he taught them in an open field. The class grew larger and larger. Petero was very busy. Soon he almost forgot that he was ill.

Molokai—land of cliffs—was the plain sister of the beautiful Hawaiian family of islands, which are really a range of volcanic mountains thousands of years old. From the time their sharp peaks had first risen from beneath the Pacific Ocean, Molokai had known a certain loneliness. The early Polynesian people who lived in the Hawaiian Islands, as well as later settlers from many parts of the world, did not find on Molokai the peculiar magic, the enchantment of the other islands. Her coasts, harborless and rocky, did not beckon the passing ships to linger.

Especially forbidding was that finger of land on which Damien now found himself and that ran into the ocean on the northern end of the island. It was about six miles square, surrounded on three sides by water and on the fourth by the *palis*. No better place to isolate the sick could have been chosen by the Hawaiian government, for escape was almost impossible.

Nor did Molokai enjoy the sunny, mild climate typical of the rest of Hawaii. The towering *palis* served as a wall to the prevailing winds sweeping in over the shore, bringing cold and drenching rain down upon those who cowered in its shadows, unprotected by warm clothing or even a decent roof. The poor people, already weakened by disease, had no resistance to these conditions and suffered greatly from exposure and chill. Added to this was the fact that the government food supply was far from sufficient. Six dollars a year was given each person for clothing. Very little interest was shown in their welfare. It was easy for government officials in Honolulu to forget those whom they had sent into exile.

It took Damien only a few days in his new parish to see all these things. He saw that, although he had come to them as a priest, he must also serve as doctor, for there was none. He must turn carpenter once more if they were to have houses and churches. He must be their spokesman to the outside world if they were to obtain food, clothing, and other necessities.

He always carried his rosary, praying it alone, with the sick in their huts, and with the children who clustered around him. He found he must also carry his hammer, the necessary tool of building. That was how the people soon grew used to seeing their priest, striding around the settlement with his rosary and hammer always in hand, and nearly always in use.

The colony was seven years old and had about eight hundred patients when Damien arrived. Damien was thirty-three years old—the age of Christ at the crucifixion. Strong and fearless, full of hope, he went to work.

"Petero," Damien said one day, "how would you like to have a real house to live in?"

Petero looked surprised. "You mean, Kamiano, like the one you had at Vaiapuka?"

"Much better than that one, Petero", Damien answered firmly. "The government has sent over lumber. I'm going to start building some nice cottages here today."

Kaimu ran to bring Kamiano's hammer and saw. He was never far from Damien's side and liked to help him do his work.

"Come now, Kaimu, let's be off", Damien said briskly. He had a plan in mind. Already he could see the row of neat, white cottages he would put up, each one standing on trestles to keep it off the damp ground, and each one with its little garden of vegetables and flowers. He was teaching Kaimu how to use the hammer, too. Soon the boy would be a valuable assistant. And others wanted to learn also. Between them they would get things done!

Outside the narrow limits of the colony, the news that a young Catholic priest had gone to stay at Molokai quickly attracted public notice. Only a few days after his going there, the Honolulu newspaper *Nuhou* ran a story under the heading "A Christian Hero".

"We have often said", the article stated, "that the poor outcasts of Molokai, without pastor or physician, afforded an opportunity for the exercise of a noble Christian heroism, and we are happy to say that the hero has been found." It went on to tell the story of Damien.

When word of this sudden fame reached Damien, he dismissed it sharply: "If they saw how things really are here, they wouldn't talk like that!"

His only wish was to be allowed to remain and to do what he could to help. But it was not to be his decision alone!

Everyone thought he had gone to Molokai to stay, but Bishop Maigret had had no such intention. The vicar apostolic had sent him there as a temporary measure to ease a critical situation. Other priests were equally willing to share responsibility for this mission. After several months, when Bishop Maigret saw the good results of Damien's work, he gave him permission to remain. Thus Damien became the pastor of the Catholics at Molokai with the full agreement of his superiors.

But, as he was not himself a victim of the disease, he was bound under Hawaiian law to obtain government permission to stay at Molokai. The Honolulu board of health, in charge of affairs at the colony, had been growing much stricter about allowing well persons to visit the island. They wished to prevent the further spread of the disease.

Some members of the board of health, composed largely of ministers of other faiths, were not in favor of Damien's staying at the colony, perhaps partly because he was being given such wide public acclaim. To force him to leave, they issued an order forbidding him to come to Honolulu for any reason. Now he was a prisoner. Surely he would resent that and decide to escape from Molokai.

But he accepted the order. The thought of leaving never came to him.

What hurt Damien most was the fact that he could no longer go to the mainland for confession, nor could a priest visit him. The necessity of going for months at a time without the sacrament of penance was one of the sharpest sufferings he was to endure. If he dared to leave Molokai's shores, he would be arrested as a common criminal. Now that he had chosen exile, he was to share the outcast's every sorrow.

Father Modeste, provincial of the Sacred Hearts Fathers in Honolulu, knew how Damien felt. One day he decided to go to Kalaupapa on the island steamer, at least to hear Damien's confession.

As the sick were being unloaded on the beach, amid the usual cries and moans, Father Modeste started down the gangplank. The ship's captain was at his side in a moment. His voice was harsh.

"Wait! I have orders to stop you. You can't go ashore."

Father Modeste looked up in surprise.

"Why not?"

The captain did not want to waste words in an unpleasant task.

"Because, if you do, I shall have to turn you over to the police", he answered shortly, placing himself right in Father Modeste's path.

"You mean I will be arrested?" asked Father Modeste.

"You'd better not try to land", repeated the captain.

Damien, who was standing on the shore, watching,

jumped into a small boat and rowed out to the side of the *Mokili*. As he made ready to go on board to meet his superior, the captain again spoke.

"If you come on board this ship, I shall have to arrest you, too."

Damien hesitated only a moment. Above him, Father Modeste stood at the ship's rail. Closer than this they could not be. Soon the *Mokili* would turn and head outward again, bearing Father Modeste back to Honolulu and leaving Damien alone once more. Weeks, months, might pass with no other priest daring to defy the government order.

Damien called to the captain. "Do you speak French?"

"No." The captain was puzzled. He did not like this business at all. He was merely carrying out orders. The sooner he could get away from Kalaupapa, the more pleased he would be!

Damien called up to him again. "Your crew—do they understand French?"

"No." The same answer once again.

Turning to Father Modeste, Damien's voice rang out again over the clear water.

"Then, Father, will you hear my confession here?"

Father Modeste slipped his stole over his traveling clothes and stood attentively looking down at the figure in the small boat below. The captain and crew members turned away. They pretended to be very busy about their duties on the ship.

"Bless me, Father, for I have sinned . . ."

The French words spoken in Damien's powerful voice traveled out in all directions, as if borne on the water. Soon Father Modeste's hand was seen as he gave the absolution.

Damien immediately sat down in his boat and started back to shore. He rowed swiftly, without once turning around.

The *Mokili* stood only a little longer offshore and then moved out toward the blue and open water. Damien returned to his work with a new peace after his strange confession on the sea.

Later, through the influence of the French consul, the ruling of the board of health was somewhat eased "to admit the visits of medical men and ministers of religion for the exercise of the functions of their office, provided they have previously obtained special permission". Damien obtained the necessary authorization and thereafter could leave the colony on business.

Although officially his duties were to minister to the souls of the sick, the terrible physical conditions he found forced him to do much more. The Hawaiian government had placed a superintendent in charge of the colony, but this official did not actually live at the settlement. Some of the patients had more or less official positions, but the others had little confidence in them. The government failed not only to provide fair and responsible supervision but also to supply the food, clothing, shelter, and medical supplies so desperately needed. Damien did his best to make up for all these shortcomings. In the years to come, his efforts on rare occasions brought him into conflict with government authorities. For the most part, mutual cooperation and friendship existed between them.

Besides the cottages, Damien needed also to build churches and a home for Kaimu and his friends. After some weeks, Damien had built for himself a log house. It was small, measuring only twelve by fifteen feet. Next to him would be the boys' home, so that he could watch over them and see that they were well cared for. Then there must be a home for girls, too, and someone to look after them. Kiulia, a kind Hawaiian woman who had come to Molokai to nurse the ill, would take care of his children.

His own door was hardly ever closed. Even at night, people came looking for him.

When he came to Molokai, he had found on the lips of many of its people an ugly phrase: *Aole kanawai ma reia wahi!* "In this place there is no law!"

Now this was being replaced by another: "If we need anything, we go to Makua Kamiano, and he helps us."

Damien had written to the good Sisters of the Sacred Hearts at Honolulu, asking them to send whatever they could spare. With their generous gifts, he opened up a regular warehouse that quickly became famous throughout the settlement for its wonderful treasures.

There they would find the priest, sleeves rolled up, a cheerful word for everyone, passing out gifts—bread, biscuits, rice, sugar, eggs, candy, and clothes.

One dark night, when the rain was falling heavily, Kaimu knocked on Damien's door.

"Oh, Kamiano, someone calls for you, someone very sick . . ."

Damien was putting on his coat as Kaimu told him of the woman on the other side of the settlement. He must ride quickly. He saddled his patient horse and led it into the drenching downpour. He knew the place. The woman was a Christian, but she had not been to church in many years. He urged his horse forward through the mud and darkness. He must be there in time, for he knew she was now very ill.

Outside her hut, he hitched his horse carefully. His coat, thrown over the saddle, would help protect the animal while he was gone. The horse whinnied and pawed the slippery earth.

Inside, Damien found a group of Catholic women gathered around the sick one. They stepped back as Damien went to speak to her. As he anointed her, they began to pray aloud. The woman had made a good confession. Now she was at peace.

In a little while, Damien went out to find his horse and go home. No horse! Upset by the storm, it had somehow broken its halter and run off. And not only that! Damien's coat, fastened to the saddle, was gone with it. In the pitch blackness of the night, there was no use trying to find the horse. He could hardly see a foot in front of him. There was nothing to do but to set out walking through the mud and rain, drenched to the skin.

The horse and coat might be lost forever, but the soul had been saved! He hardly minded the chill and wetness as he trudged back to his Kalawao house.

Sometimes, on his many trips around the settlement, he would hear the muffled beat of the *uli-uli* drums, signal for the old religious rites, still practiced by some Hawaiians. They would perform the traditional hula dances in honor of the pagan god Laka. Often these celebrations led to great excesses on the part of some of the people, especially when they were accompanied by large quantities of *ki*, the powerful drink made from the roots of plants that grew on the lower reaches of the *palis*.

Damien had little patience with those who tried, by ignoring law and order, to break down the already discouraged spirits of his people. With his stout cane, he would stride straight into the group of troublemakers, looking very fierce indeed. Usually he had only to make his appearance to put things to rights again. Even the most lawless never offered to oppose him by any sort of violence, and gradually even those few were won over by his unfailing charity and hard work.

Many things were changing at Molokai since Damien had come. The people had even begun to find their voices again.

"I'll know my work is succeeding when I hear them start to sing", Damien thought. Elsewhere in the islands he had always heard Hawaiians singing. Music was in their hearts, music and happiness.

"Kaimu," Damien called one day as he saw the boy pass his house, "get some of the boys. I have an idea."

Kaimu went running. Kamiano's ideas were always good. The priest had gone off in the other direction, his long black cassock flapping with his big steps.

The boys were waiting impatiently before the log house when Damien came back, carrying the strangest assortment of things. Pieces of wood, left-over tin, odds and ends of building materials. He tossed them down into a clattering pile.

"We're going to have a band!" he announced cheerfully. "Come on, now, each one of you pick an instrument, and we'll start practice."

"Instruments?" Kaimu laughed. "But Kamiano, we have no instruments at all."

"Right before you", Damien replied. He picked up a piece of pipe and experimented with blowing across it. The boys now had the idea. Musical talent was in every one of them. From the crude materials at hand, they managed to make primitive instruments. That is how the famous Molokai band came to be. After that, it played for all feast days and other important occasions. Some kind persons in Honolulu later collected the money for a beautiful set of real band instruments. Costumes were made from the old drapes that had once hung in Saint Philomena's.

As the great Feast of Corpus Christi came near, there were many excited preparations. Damien thought of the wonderful parades and fairs that always marked the holy days of Belgium. Why should his Hawaiians, who also loved colorful celebrations, not enjoy a similar happiness?

The High Mass on the morning of Corpus Christi was a splendid occasion. The newly organized choir, in its bright-colored robes, sang beautifully.

When he rose to give the sermon, Damien spoke as if he were one of those afflicted ones who listened so intently to his words. Never did he use the terms "I" and "you"—always "we". Again, as always, he spoke of eternal hope.

"Earth is only a place we are passing through, an exile", he said. "Heaven is our real homeland. We are sure of going there soon, and there we shall be repaid for all our suffering. The more patiently we bear our troubles here, the more beautiful and joyful we shall be there!"

Beauty of face and form was sadly missing in the congregation that had gathered that morning at the sound of the church bell. But beauty of soul was there. The marks of death were on their bodies, but the brightness of life eternal illuminated their hearts. And Damien was happy, because he had brought them hope.

That afternoon, the Corpus Christi procession began. They had prepared two repositories draped with the Hawaiian national colors, one in the hospital yard, one near the shore. The stronger men had brought down bamboo from the mountain to make the canopy and altar, and the children had wound the branches with red and white paper. The women had worked for days cutting up the old church drapes, making big and bright banners.

Petero led the procession, carrying the cross. After him came the children and younger people, gaily dressed in costumes. Then came the altar, followed by the choirs singing the hymn *Lauda Sion* with brave gusto.

Little girls dressed in blue and white carried baskets of flowers to cover the path with petals. Kaimu and three other boys served as acolytes. They carried flags. Four men in green uniforms bore the canopy under which Damien walked, carrying the Blessed Sacrament.

He walked very, very slowly, timing his pace with those who could barely manage to take a step, for everyone able to move had come today. Even non-Catholics were following the procession. There was a great spirit of happiness and enthusiasm everywhere. One would have thought, perhaps, that these were the most joyful people in the world.

But on Damien's face, as he held aloft the monstrance, there were tears!

11

THE ENEMY STRIKES BACK

T HE YEARS since Damien's coming had brought great
changes to Molokai. Kaimu was a young man now,
a prayer leader like Petero. Although he could not run
anymore, or even walk very well, Kaimu remained
Damien's loyal friend and helper. As for Petero, the
trouble was mostly with his eyes, but he never lost his

happy disposition. He was always either busy about Saint Philomena's or teaching the children. Other boys kept coming to join Damien's big "family". Some of the sick children came from the boat carrying notes to Makua Kamiano, asking him to look after them.

The two settlements of Kalawao and Kalaupapa were like small villages anywhere in Hawaii. A good road had been built connecting them, and along the road people rode horseback, went to market and to school, and delivered food and other supplies in oxcarts. A path had been cut over the *palis*, too, and, while the sick did not venture to cross it, it helped take away their sense of utter desolation.

Life at Molokai was life anywhere, with its share of work and play, joy and sorrow. If there was a little more of the sorrow, faith enabled the people to make the best of it. Farming and other industry flourished. From one end of the peninsula to the other, the bells of the two churches Damien had built answered one another's call.

Damien could see all around him the results of his work. He could look back upon moments of great happiness, as well as moments of great discouragement.

On a September day in 1881, they had had a visit from Princess Liliuokalani, sister of King Kalakua. Because she was acting as ruler of Hawaii in the absence of the king, she was called Queen Liliuokalani.

The steamer *Lehua* anchored at Kalaupapa. Boats decorated with many flowers brought the queen and her party ashore. There they found a wonderful welcome waiting for them. About eight hundred people gathered on the shore. They watched Queen Liliuokalani as she left the wharf and started down the flower-covered path to a specially built platform under a large tent. An honor guard of seventy persons in uniforms escorted the ruler under gaily decorated arches.

The queen was a kind-hearted woman, much loved by her people. They waited excitedly as she took her place on the stage in her long black robe. All around her stood officials and ladies-in-waiting.

Just then, the girls' choir of Molokai began to sing for the queen a beautiful Hawaiian song. They were wearing lovely white dresses with red or blue sashes. Everything had been planned days ahead for this event. Never before had the colony received so distinguished a visitor. In fact, any visitor at all was a rare occasion there!

As the queen smiled down on the singers and the crowd before her, she suddenly noticed someone she knew—first one, then another. She looked about, and the smile slowly left her face. Yes, there were quite a few whom she could remember from happier days. When she saw how the disease had affected them, her kind heart grew sad, and she began to cry. Her ladies-in-waiting and all her attendants began to cry, too. As the song ended, there were tears all around. This was not the way Damien had planned things at all. He wanted it to be a happy and gala day for everyone.

Queen Liliuokalani began to speak, but she could not overcome her feeling of sorrow and shock. Kapena, the prime minister, finally stepped forward and gave the speech for her. It was very moving.

After the formal ceremonies, Damien and the officials in charge of the colony took Queen Liliuokalani on a tour of the settlement. She was very much interested and wanted to see everything during her short visit. Try as she might, however, she could not quite forget her sadness of the morning.

That evening, when it was time to leave, Queen Liliuokalani and her company once more boarded their ship. She went back quite brokenhearted. Many of those who had come with her had found at Molokai some relative or friend from whom they had long been separated. Mothers had visited a little while with their children. Now they had to leave them again.

Queen Liliuokalani thanked Damien for all he had done to help the people of Molokai. When she went home, she did not forget them but sent gifts of clothing and other things. She gave Damien a decoration and made him a knight commander of the Royal Order of Kalakua. Damien accepted the title graciously. The people were happy to see their pastor so honored and begged him to wear his decoration.

After the first day, when he had worn it to please them, Damien put the honor away in the drawer of his desk and did not put it on again.

"It doesn't look right on this ragged old cassock", he would say laughingly whenever they asked him about it.

*   *   *

For the last twenty years or so of his life, Damien kept a notebook. In it he wrote his rule of life, the one he had learned as a young student in the Congregation of the Sacred Hearts, which he had kept faithfully. In this book he also wrote out ideas for sermons and his own thoughts from day to day. After all, he had no one to speak to of his own trials or of his dearest hopes.

As he went about, with his hammer in one hand and his rosary in the other, he always appeared jolly. But, even for one of his joyous nature, there were moments of terrible loneliness. No fellow priest was near to share his burdens or even, for long periods, to hear his confession. Year after year passed, and Damien fought on, always alone.

"May all the honor, all the praise they can give to me, return to God, whose servant I am!" he had written in his book.

His greatest happiness was to see his children—the boys and girls whom he had taken under his care. Each day he spent several hours with them.

Each morning after Mass and his breakfast of rice, meat, coffee, and rolls, he would call out, "Who's coming with me?"

Many of the boys became good carpenters, helping him with the building They followed him around the settlement all day, hammering and sawing away side by side with him,

They liked to go with him to the churchyard, when he fed his flock of chickens. Here, for a few minutes, he would become once more a farmer of Flanders, scattering a few grains of corn on the ground and calling his flock with a strange little cry. Instantly they would come, on foot and wing, like a cloud around him. They would sit on his shoulders and eat from his hands.

Sometime each day he would visit the hospital, where the worst cases were. Bringing his gifts and medicine, he would listen to each one's troubles. Often he would take the broom and begin to sweep and clean. Whatever had to be done he would do cheerfully. While he worked, he would tell stories or sing songs to amuse the patients.

For some time he had acted as a doctor at the settlement, for there had been none at Molokai for many years. When doctors came, in later years, they were surprised to find the priest quite expert at treating the sick. After long hours of this, he would return to the children. Out into the garden they would go.

"Now I'll show you how to keep the bugs off these cabbages", Damien would say, scattering cinders along the row. With his help, they planted radishes, carrots, turnips, and other vegetables, even banana trees!

Sometimes the seeds for these came from faraway America. Damien had somehow found time to look through catalogues and send away to the United States for plants he thought would grow in Molokai's rather hard, volcanic soil.

One day, he came into the yard leading a young colt he had bought on the other side of the island.

"See what I have for you!" he called out happily.

"Now, come on, one of you, and have a ride." He was often seen breaking in ponies for them.

As for food, he saw to it that they had the very best. His sharp peasant eye saw the good use of everything. An old hardened piece of lava became a wonderful oven for baking bread.

"This oven of yours would be the envy of any baker in the world!" he would tell them proudly.

And then, each evening, after his meal, which usually was leftovers warmed over a small lamp, he would sit with them by the hour. They would talk and sing, and he would teach them a new catechism lesson.

As the night came, the voices of the children, high-pitched and happy, would be heard in the dusk, saying the Rosary with the priest.

"One more song, and then to bed!" he would tell them. For them, the day was done. For him, there might be many more hours of sick calls, instruction, labor, prayer.

Every morning they would all meet again at Saint Philomena's for the early Mass. They would recite together the catechism lesson of the night before. They were as happy as any big family. When they came to die, he was at their side.

"My children die like saints", he said again and again. He had prepared them well for heaven.

He seemed to be tireless. His face was tanned, his step strong and quick, his eyes steady as ever, twinkling as usual behind his gold-rimmed glasses. But his feet had begun to bother him a great deal after his long day. They burned at night. No wonder, for he was on them too much!

One evening in December 1884, he put his aching feet into some water to ease the pain. In a very few minutes, red blisters began to appear on them. He put his hand into the water to feel its temperature. It was almost boiling! Still, his feet were numb. He felt no pain at all!

This lack of feeling, he knew, was one of the signs of *maipake*. Exactly when it had begun, no one knew for sure. There had been little hints that the enemy illness was beginning to attack him. But it had come slowly. Now it made its presence felt beyond any doubt.

The next day, Damien went to the doctor at the settlement.

"I can't bear to tell you—but it's true", said the doctor sadly.

"I already know", was Damien's firm answer.

He wrote to Father Pamphile about this news.

"There is no more doubt about me. I have leprosy. Blessed be the good God!"

Again he spoke of it to his brother—"Having no doubts about the true nature of my disease, I am calm, resigned, and very happy in the midst of my people."

He told someone, "I would not want to be cured if it meant leaving the island."

But there was no question of a cure. So far, none had been found!

Back in Tremeloo, Mrs. de Veuster was now very old. Damien had always written to her faithfully, even though it was hard for him to remember the Flemish words he had not spoken in so many years. He did not tell her of his illness, for he wished to spare her this terrible knowledge

The news, however, had spread very quickly. Newspapers all over the world, which had begun to follow Damien's work with interest, splashed the story of his affliction in big headlines. Some went so far as to draw a grim picture of his condition, which was not true to the facts at all. In this way, Mrs. de Veuster learned that her son had leprosy.

"Well, then," she said calmly, "I will go with him to heaven." She turned to his picture, which she always kept beside her bed. A few days later, she did go to heaven, content that she would meet her Joseph there.

Damien's feet now bothered him so much that he could not walk around the island or even ride his horse. He made his usual rounds in an old battered wagon, instead. It was his custom always to meet the boat when it came. Quite often it carried supplies for his work or sick people who needed help right away.

One day, he saw a tall man walk ashore with the firm step of a soldier. The man, dressed in a plain, neat, blue denim suit, came right over to where Damien sat, holding the reins in his wagon.

"I'm Joseph Dutton", the stranger said. "I've come to help you in any way I can."

With this simple statement, the man who was to be Damien's friend and helper and who was to carry on his work for many years, took his place in the wagon. Damien's worn face lit up with joy. Here, at last, was the one he had waited for for so long.

As they drove back to the settlement, Joseph Dutton told his story. It was a short one. He never liked to say much about himself.

An American and a former army officer, Joseph Dutton had chosen a life of dedication and penance. After spending some time with the Trappist monks, he had decided his vocation was not there. While sitting in the library of the house of the Redemptorist priests in New Orleans, he had glanced through an old newspaper and read a piece about Molokai. That immediately made up his mind. He would go there and devote his life to service of the sick.

"There's so much to be done, Brother Joseph", Damien told him. "Right now, I want to rebuild our church, Saint Philomena's. It is not big enough anymore to hold everyone who comes to Mass. Besides, a windstorm has blown down the steeple."

A Protestant minister in England, Reverend Chapman, took up a collection and sent Damien the money, given by both Catholics and non-Catholics. In his letter, Reverend Chapman, who had been for a long time a loyal contributor to Damien's work, said: "I herewith send you . . . a thousand pounds, which has been subscribed by many who are grateful to God for the example of your heroic self-devotion. Personally, I have done nothing in the matter, except receive the funds, and I require no thanks whatever. The honor is with those who are thus allowed to testify to you their respectful love."

Reverend Chapman also told Damien that the money was to be used for the building of a church for the Catholics of Molokai.

"This time we'll use stone instead of wood", Damien told his helpers. "We can quarry it right here. This way we need not buy materials, and, besides, the stone will last longer." He was right, for this church is still standing and may be seen by travelers to Molokai today.

For many years, Damien had Perpetual Adoration of the Blessed Sacrament in both churches at the settlement. It was a devotion dear to him as a member of the Fathers of the Sacred Hearts. Even the sick took turns watching in church during the long night hours.

The name of Damien was now known the world over.

"Voyagers of all nations," someone had written in a European newspaper, "salute when you pass the cliffs of Molokai!"

For those who actually stopped to see the famous priest, a big surprise was waiting. They found, not a hero at all, but a man in working clothes on the roof of Saint Philomena's, hammering away happily with his calloused, workworn hands.

12

ALOHA KAMIANO

FROM THE beginning of his priesthood, Damien's life had been one of sacrifice. He was used to that. It did not surprise him that God should now ask of him the last, the final, surrender. He had long been ready to make it.

From boyhood, Damien had been blessed with unusual health and strength. His body had been that of an athlete—powerful, disciplined, handsome. He might have been proud of it. Instead, he had used it solely for God's purposes.

Now he saw that it must be destroyed to make his life of self-surrender complete. Sickness and physical weakness had been unknown to him until now. But when the disease came, it struck a vicious blow. Other men, being weaker at the start, leprosy might destroy slowly. But in Damien's case, all the destructive forces of disease rushed in with stunning speed. Within the short space of five years, Damien, the giant, was brought down. His body was a ruin, like that of Christ on Calvary.

It seemed almost as if the sickness wanted revenge from this man because he had defied it, holding eternal hope before its grinning death's head of despair.

He went on with his work at a feverish pace. He knew he had not much time left. He wanted to leave nothing undone that might be done for his people.

His one great sorrow was that he might die before anyone came to carry on his work. He could not bear to leave his children twice orphaned. That seemed to be all that kept him going.

At last, on November 14, 1888, three angels appeared at Kalaupapa! At any rate, to Damien's failing eyesight they looked like angels, though they wore the habit of the Franciscan Sisters of Syracuse, New York. They had come to look after his children.

The priest, who had been too weak to leave his room for six weeks, made the great effort of driving over to

Kalaupapa to welcome the sisters. Mother Marianne and two of her nuns, Sister Leopoldina and Sister Vincentia, had come on the boat from Honolulu.

Damien took them to see the home he had built for the girls at Kalawao. As the children ran to gather around him, he spoke to them in his usual direct way.

"My children, I am going to die soon, but you will not be forgotten. These good sisters you see here have come to take care of you. Go back with them now to your new home at Kalaupapa!"

They all began to cry. Damien was, after all, the only guardian they had ever known. The nuns in their habits looked strange. But when Mother Marianne began to speak to the children gently, all but two gradually allowed themselves to be led away.

These clung to Damien's feet, crying, "No, no, Kamiano! We want to stay as long as you are here." The sisters had to go back without them.

For Damien, the coming of the sisters to Molokai was a gift from heaven. For many years he had begged the bishop to send them, but until that time it was not customary to allow women to risk contagion with this particular disease.

Mother Marianne was a wonderful woman. She brought to the last days of Damien and to the children he was leaving a much-needed warmth of love and understanding and, at the same time, a great deal of very practical ability.

"My day is done", Damien told this courageous

woman. "Now I can go in peace. You will care for my children even better than I could do."

Two priests, Father Wendelin and Father Conrardy, had also come to assist at the settlement.

Damien had tried various treatments suggested by friends the world over, but it was now quite clear that nothing could slow down the rapid progress of his illness. For a time he grew sad and quiet. He wondered whether his sacrifice would win him a place in heaven. The overwhelming loneliness of all his priestly years suddenly seemed to crowd upon him in his weakness and pain. This was only a passing trial, however. Then he was up and out again, remembering many things he had still to do. Brother Dutton followed him around faithfully each day, taking up each task where Damien had to leave it, helping him to finish before his working day was done. Damien thought most often of the children. He tried to make toys for them, a hobby he had never had enough time for before.

During the winter, an English artist named Edward Clifford came for a visit at Molokai. Though not a Catholic, Clifford had been for many years a great admirer of Damien's courage, and he wished to meet the priest.

In the harbor at Kalaupapa, the seas were very rough. Clifford's ship had to go on to Kalawao. In a small boat, the visitor tried to reach a rocky promontory not too far from the settlement. After a while, the water grew a little calmer, and Clifford and his party managed to reach the shore. Damien was waiting with about twenty people on the foam-laced beach, his big straw hat on his head and on his face a beaming smile.

"Edward!" He reached over and took the younger man's hand in a warm greeting. The children gathered around and watched with great curiosity as Clifford unloaded his cargo of gifts from England. A number of wealthy and notable persons had contributed offerings for Damien and his people. There were paintings and other works of art, medicines, and a magic lantern, with a set of slides showing biblical scenes.

Most wonderful of all, Clifford unwrapped a hand organ. This had been sent by Lady Caroline Charteris, he told Damien, and you could play as many as forty tunes on it by merely turning the crank.

Soon Damien was showing the boys how to use it, and after that there were very few times when the hand organ could not be heard somewhere around Kalawao. Lady Caroline had chosen her gift well!

As for Clifford himself, he asked nothing but the privilege of painting Damien's portrait.

"It's the one favor I ask of you", he told the priest earnestly.

Damien laughed. "I don't think I will be such a good model just now, but if that's what you wish, go ahead."

They sat long hours on the upstairs balcony of Damien's house, with the leaves of the fragrant honeysuckle shading them. As the artist worked, the priest said his breviary or spoke about his work. He recalled for Clifford many events of the sixteen years he had been at

Molokai. Clifford was delighted to listen. Later on, he wrote a book describing Damien for others who would never meet him in person. The priest's voice was now much affected by his illness, yet he sang a song for his guest. In Damien's workroom, Clifford saw the shelves of books, spiritual writings by which the solitary missionary had guided his own difficult life.

Clifford walked around the island and looked closely at the three hundred neat, whitewashed cottages, with their little gardens, nestling at the foot of the black *palis*. He wanted to see and remember everything for the book he was planning.

"Would you like to see your portrait?" Clifford asked, when he had finished his painting.

"What an ugly face!" Damien exclaimed. "I did not know the disease had gone so far."

"Shall I send this to your brother, Father Pamphile?" Clifford wanted to know.

"Please don't do that", Damien answered quickly. "It would hurt him too much to see me this way."

When Clifford was leaving, the priest gave him a little card of flowers from Jerusalem. On the flyleaf of Clifford's Bible, he wrote simply, "I was sick, and you visited me." But by far the greatest gift Clifford carried back with him to England was the memory of a great and humble man who had no idea of his own heroism.

One day, Damien took up his pen to write again to Mount Saint Anthony, now a fading memory of his seminary years. Father Pamphile, the professor, the student, had never, after all, taken that long hoped-for journey around Cape Horn to join his brother in the Hawaiian mission. Many years had passed, and the two priest brothers from Tremeloo had not met again. Their paths had led in very different ways, yet they remained close in the bonds of their brotherhood, both family and religious.

"To my dear brother . . ." Damien wrote now with difficulty, for his hands were swollen and covered with sores.

> Considering the disease that the Good Lord has seen fit to send me, I do not write you as I used to do. . . . I am continually happy and, though very ill, I wish for nothing but the fulfillment of the holy will of God. . . .
>
> Will you greet for me all the Fathers and Brothers of Louvain, as well as Gerard, Leonce, and the whole family? At Mass, which up to now I have been able to say every day (though with a certain difficulty), I do not forget any of you. Will you, in return, pray and have prayers said for me as I drag myself slowly toward the grave? May the good Lord strengthen me and give me the grace of perseverance and of a good death. . . .
>
> Your devoted brother in the Sacred Hearts,
>
> J. Damien de Veuster

Finally, he had to stop working. He lay very ill on the floor of his room. Brother James Sinnott, who had been a nurse and had recently come, like Brother Dutton, to help at the settlement, could find no sheets or anything else to make the sick man more comfortable. Damien had received so many of these things through the years and had given every one of them away. Somewhere they found a bed and persuaded him to rest on it instead of on the floor.

During the day, he liked to have them carry him to the little patch of grass in front of his house. There the people would gather around him, hour after hour, talking or chanting softly to pass away the time.

The Feast of Saint Joseph came. It was exactly twenty-five years since young Brother Damien had first seen Honolulu harbor on his voyage from Europe. His memory went back to that day, so long ago, when he had said good-bye to his mother at the shrine of Our Lady of Montaigu. Twelve years he had prayed for that day— twelve years to spend himself in the missions! God had been good. He had been given twenty-five!

The light hurt his eyes, but he did not want to give up saying his breviary. As he lay there through the long night hours, his failing sight and failing strength leaving him at times in a strange world of shadows, he sometimes thought he was back in Belgium.

He saw again in the distance the magnificent tower of Saint Rombaut's, like lacework made of stone. How near it seemed to him now! Yes, he could almost hear the glorious pealing of the bells. It was evening, and the sheep and cows would be nodding in the pastures at

Tremeloo. The bell *was* ringing, certainly. It seemed to come closer, closer.

It was the tiny tinkle of the Communion bell. Father Wendelin and Father Conrardy were beginning their nightly procession through the darkened house to bring him Holy Communion at midnight.

He turned to Brother Dutton beside him.

"How long will it be?" he whispered again.

"By Easter it will be over", came the same gentle answer.

The glorious Feast of the Resurrection was drawing nearer. Damien was always happy and at peace. He had received the Last Rites and had renewed his vows in the Congregation of the Sacred Hearts.

"How good God is", he told those around him, "to have made me live long enough to see at this moment two priests at my side and the Franciscan Sisters at the settlement! I can sing *Nunc Dimittis*. My work is in good hands. And I—I am no longer necessary. I am going to heaven!"

"When you are there, Father Damien," one of the sisters said, "you won't forget those whom you are leaving behind, will you?"

"Oh, no! If I have any power with God, I will intercede for everyone here", he answered.

Father Wendelin spoke next.

"Leave me your cloak, Father Damien," he begged, "just as Elijah gave his cloak to Elisha, so that he might inherit his great heart."

Damien brushed aside this idea, as he had always brushed aside any reference to his own greatness.

"What, that old thing! What could you do with it? Anyhow, it's probably full of germs."

"Then give me your blessing, Father", the younger priest asked.

"That I do, my son, with all my heart!" Tears came to Damien's eyes as he tried to lift his hand in the Sign of the Cross. After that, he blessed the sisters and asked Father Wendelin to say with him the prayers of his community.

"How sweet it is to die a child of the Sacred Hearts!" he exclaimed thankfully.

Around his doorway the people of the settlement kept constant watch. Years before, a poet of Molokai had composed a hymn expressing all the sad longing of the sick for the end of their exile. It was their chant of departure. They sang it for him now.

> *When, oh, when shall it be given to me*
> *To behold my God?*
> *How long shall I be captive in this strange land . . .*

On the eve of Palm Sunday he received Communion for the last time. The people watching saw once again the flicker of candles carried through the peaceful house.

Very early the next morning, as the gray shadows of the *palis* had begun to lift, Damien's soul took its way out of that valley of death. A soul of fire and restless drive, it now left on its heavenly flight as gently as that of a child.

In the misty morning, the news went out that Kami-ano had gone. The people sat on the ground, beating their breasts in old Hawaiian fashion, swaying back and forth, and wailing sadly. Others might come now. The bars of their prison had been pried open. But Kamiano would not come again. The bell of Saint Philomena's tolled slowly, sending out its sorrowful message across the water.

All signs of illness had gone from his face, and his hands were completely healed. Later, his body lay in the church he had built with those hands, before the altar where he had so often offered the Holy Sacrifice for those he loved.

The next day, after the funeral Mass, there was a great procession, just like the many he had held for the people through the years. They put on their festal costumes and bore their bright banners. The band played better than ever before.

As he had asked, they laid his body at the foot of the old pandanus tree, his first home at Molokai, where he had slept on the night of his coming. Petero led the way there, carrying the cross, as usual. This time, he was guided by the limping Kaimu, for Petero could not see to find his way alone anymore.

Mother Marianne came and gently led away the two little girls who had refused to leave Father Damien. They went with her willingly now.

Kaimu helped the younger boys plant white flowers all around the old tree. When the day ended, many were still there. They sang the ancient Hawaiian song of sad farewell, "Aloha Kamiano . . ."

It was not for him that they were grieving. He had gone to heaven, whose glories he had so often promised them. They had been left behind.

The white flowers blossomed there for forty-six years, while the story of Damien de Veuster was carried to every part of the world. In 1936, King Leopold of Belgium arranged for the body of Damien to be returned to his homeland. On the Belgian ship *Mercator*, attended by many honors from San Francisco to Antwerp, it was brought back. There it was met by King Leopold, the cardinal primate of Belgium, and many other high officials of Church and state.

Guns fired salutes as the carriage, drawn by six white horses, wound to the public square. The humble and the great came to pay homage. And the bells rang, this time for him, the bells of his own country in the church towers he had always loved.

Later, the body was placed in a special car to be taken to its final resting place at Louvain. There, Damien's missionary dream had come to him. From there, he had gone forth to make his heroic sacrifice.

In the silence of night, the procession wound through the Belgian countryside, through Damien's quiet native village of Tremeloo. Down the familiar roads the priest had known so well, between fields where he had played or tended flocks, the strange parade passed. Everyone in Tremeloo was out, standing along the way. As the car went by, they knelt by the roadside. Some members of the de Veuster family were there, as Damien passed his home on earth for the last time.

In the tower of Saint Rombaut's, the bells spoke again over the listening fields. They might tell, this time, the story that began within the sound of their own voices. The great bell named Salvator boomed in triumph, for the Flemish boy who had given everything—even his life—for his brothers in Christ.

On the great doors of Saint Peter's in Rome an announcement has been posted. The investigation that may lead to the canonization of Damien de Veuster has begun. The world will rejoice even more when and if his name is added to the great list of the saints.

If Damien himself were to return to Molokai today, he would rejoice. Things are very different there. No more the bleak and terrible scenes he found on that day in 1873 when he first stepped ashore!

People now may be cured of the mysterious and once-dreaded disease and may return home to live normal lives again. Modern medicines have done much to take away the awful effects of the sickness. Those still remaining in the colony live like other people, much less handicapped than before.

Most of all, much has been done to remove the feeling of fear and disgrace that once caused the sick a mental suffering greater than any physical pain—the feeling that they were outcasts from society.

Priests, nuns, and missionaries of other faiths have devoted their life and love to the sufferers since Damien's time. Science works valiantly to study and conquer the germ that causes this disease. Even its name is changed. Now it is known as Hansen's disease, in tribute to the doctor who first discovered the nature of the infection.

It seemed to be the work of Divine Providence and grace that Damien was to be a symbol to awaken the world to the plight of these people. Even the famous letter of the Reverend C. M. Hyde, a Protestant missionary, attacking Damien after his death, had its place in the awakening. This letter, full of unjust accusations, evoked the masterful defense of Damien by another non-Catholic, the famous English author Robert Louis Stevenson. In words that fairly burn with indignation, the noted writer showed to the world the true heroism of the priest.

In his honor, the Prince of Wales, the future Edward VII of England, had a large granite cross erected at Molokai. Its inscription reads simply: "Greater love than this hath no man, that he give his life for his friend."

The great-souled Mahatma Gandhi, the Hindu religious leader, was moved to write: "The political and journalistic world can boast of very few heroes who compare with Father Damien of Molokai. The Catholic Church, on the contrary, counts by the thousands those who, after the example of Father Damien, have devoted themselves to the victims of leprosy. It is worthwhile to look for the source of such heroism."

Cardinal Pacelli (later to be Pope Pius XII) said in 1936: "The sublime devotion of this religious, consuming his life on the far-off Islands of Hawaii in the service of the lepers, to whom he abundantly gave all spiritual and corporal comforts, will remain one of the most beautiful examples of apostolic activity of our times."

Epilogue

Father Damien Joseph de Veuster took one step closer to sainthood on June 4, 1995, when Pope John Paul II beatified him during an outdoor Mass in Brussels, the capital city of Blessed Damien's home country. Before the king and queen and bishops of Belgium, as well as other civic and religious leaders, including the bishop of Honolulu, who was accompanied by delegates from the Hawaiian Islands, the Holy Father recalled the missionary priest's heroic life.

"Today, through me, the Church acknowledges and confirms the value of Fr. Damien's example along the path of holiness, praising God for having guided him to the end of his life on an often difficult journey. She joyfully contemplates what God can achieve through human weakness.

"Holiness is not perfection according to human criteria", the Pope continued; "it is not reserved for a small number of exceptional persons. It is for everyone; it is the Lord who brings us to holiness, when we are willing to collaborate in the salvation of the world for the glory of God."

The Holy Father explained that all people, in the

circumstances of their daily lives, are given opportunities to make sacrifices for the love of God and neighbor. "This is the price of true happiness", he said. "The apostle of the lepers is witness to that."

A few years after his beatification, a feast in honor of Blessed Damien Joseph de Veuster was added to the liturgical calendar in the United States. His memorial is celebrated on April 15.

Catholics are not the only Americans who celebrate the memory of Father Damien. In 1969, the state of Hawaii commemorated his life with a statue that stands in the rotunda of the United States Capitol. The bronze is based on photographs taken of Father Damien near the end of his life, when signs of leprosy were visible on his body. The statue's face is marred, and the right hand, extending from a sling, clutches a cane.

The image echoes the words prayed by Pope John Paul II at Father Damien's beatification Mass: "Blessed Damien . . . in your life and your missionary work, you show forth Christ's tenderness and mercy for every man, revealing the beauty of his inner self, which no illness, no deformity, no weakness can totally disfigure. By your actions and your preaching, you remind us that Jesus took on himself the poverty and suffering of mankind, and that he has revealed its mysterious value."

Father Damien has become a model of charity for many people throughout the world. He continues to inspire believers and non-believers who wish to imitate him and discover the source of his heroic love.

Authors' Note

The authors are indebted to those who have told the story of Father Damien before, especially John Farrow, in *Damien the Leper* (New York: Sheed and Ward), Piers Compton, in *Father Damien* (Saint Louis: Herder), and Charles J. Dutton, in *Samaritans of Molokai* (New York: Dodd, Mead).

Special thanks are due to Father Vital Jourdain, SS.CC., for the outstanding research that resulted in his book *The Heart of Father Damien*, translated into English by Father Francis Larkin, SS.CC., and Charles Davenport (Milwaukee: Bruce). This book contains records of Father Damien's life never before published, and we have relied on it as our principal source.

The Fathers of the Sacred Hearts have also assisted us, especially Father Leopold de Smet, SS.CC., founder and director of the Father Damien Institute, Tremeloo, Belgium, who very kindly sent us maps, pictures, and other valuable material. Information was also supplied by Sister Theresa Marita of the Sisters of Charity.

Accounts of Father Damien's missionary work have usually referred to the Hawaiians as a group, rather than in terms of individuals. Among the hundreds of boys Damien knew, we have chosen two as typical and have given them names. Their characters, as well as all other persons, incidents, and conversations in our story, are based upon careful study of historical records.